P9-BBN-740

His unexpected lust could get them killed.

Sutton forced his straying mind back to their still-dangerous situation. The Jeep wouldn't offer much cover if their mystery shooter sent more rounds their way.

"This doesn't make sense," Ivy said beside him. "Do you think this ambush has to do with the murders? Why lure you here and gun you down?"

"I don't know."

Ivy looked around. "You know, half the people here never lock their doors."

"That's crazy. Even in a nowhere place like Bitterwood."

"Old habits. People want to believe they're safe." She reached forward to wipe the condensation starting to fog up the windshield.

"No." Sutton grabbed her wrist, stilling the motion. She turned to look at him, her dark eyes wide with surprise. Beneath his fingers her pulse beat like the wings of a trapped bird, swift and violent.

And there it was again. Desire, licking at his belly like flames.

PAULA GRAVES

MURDER IN THE SMOKIES

HARLEQUIN® INTRIGUE®

If you purchased this book without a cover you should be aware
that this book is stolen property. It was reported as "unsold and
destroyed" to the publisher, and neither the author nor the
publisher has received any payment for this "stripped book."

For my childhood friend Julie Plant, who introduced me to the
beautiful Smoky Mountains on a trip to Lake Junaluska in western
North Carolina. We've lost touch, but I hope wherever Julie is, she gets
to see this dedication and know I remember that trip fondly,
all these years later.

ISBN-13: 978-0-373-69695-6

MURDER IN THE SMOKIES

Copyright © 2013 by Paula Graves

PLEASE RECYCLE

Recycling programs
for this product may
not exist in your area.

All rights reserved. Except for use in any review, the reproduction or
utilization of this work in whole or in part in any form by any electronic,
mechanical or other means, now known or hereafter invented, including
xerography, photocopying and recording, or in any information storage
or retrieval system, is forbidden without the written permission of the
publisher, Harlequin Enterprises Limited, 225 Duncan Mill Road,
Don Mills, Ontario M3B 3K9, Canada.

This is a work of fiction. Names, characters, places and incidents are
either the product of the author's imagination or are used fictitiously,
and any resemblance to actual persons, living or dead, business
establishments, events or locales is entirely coincidental.

This edition published by arrangement with Harlequin Books S.A.

For questions and comments about the quality of this book,
please contact us at CustomerService@Harlequin.com.

® and TM are trademarks of Harlequin Enterprises Limited or its
corporate affiliates. Trademarks indicated with ® are registered in the
United States Patent and Trademark Office, the Canadian Trade Marks
Office and in other countries.

Printed in U.S.A.

HARLEQUIN®
www.Harlequin.com

ABOUT THE AUTHOR

Alabama native Paula Graves wrote her first book, a mystery starring herself and her neighborhood friends, at the age of six. A voracious reader, Paula loves books that pair tantalizing mystery with compelling romance. When she's not reading or writing, she works as a creative director for a Birmingham advertising agency and spends time with her family and friends. She is a member of Southern Magic Romance Writers, Heart of Dixie Romance Writers and Romance Writers of America.

Paula invites readers to visit her website, www.paulagraves.com.

Books by Paula Graves

CAST OF CHARACTERS

Ivy Hawkins—The Bitterwood P.D. detective has no idea who's killing women in her small Smoky Mountain town. The last thing she needs is Sutton Calhoun breezing back into town after years away, threatening to complicate her case.

Sutton Calhoun—The son of a notorious backwoods con man left town when he realized he'd never live down his family reputation. But his security job has him back in Bitterwood, trying to solve a confounding murder.

Seth Hammond—Once Sutton's best friend, before Sutton's father took Seth under his wing and turned him into the criminal Sutton refused to be, Seth swears he's reformed his ways. But for one of the good guys, he's harboring a whole lot of secrets.

Rachel Davenport—Her father's trucking company keeps popping up in Ivy's investigation. Can the reluctant heiress help crack open a murder case?

David Pennock—The farmer claims he has a good reason for washing blood out of his rental truck while the trucking company lot is closed for the night. But does his explanation hold water?

Mark Bramlett—Though his plant nursery rents a truck from Davenport Trucking, the friendly businessman seems willing to help in any way possible. But could one of his employees have something to hide?

Captain Glen Rayburn—Ivy's superior at the Bitterwood P.D. thinks she's in over her head. But would he go so far as to sabotage her investigation?

Cleve Calhoun—Sutton's father may not be the wily old con man he used to be, but can father and son ever reconcile, or is the damage to their relationship too great?

Chapter One

People in small towns were trusting souls. Even in this wicked age, doors remained unlocked, windows unlatched behind flimsy screens designed to keep out mosquitoes and flies, not people.

Small towns made things too easy for him. They really did.

But he wasn't going to quibble about getting what he wanted without a lot of effort. He liked a challenge as much as anyone, but in the end, it was all about results.

Bitterwood, Tennessee, had sounded like exactly the place for him. One of those little Southern towns left behind by the modern world to desiccate slowly in the blazing heat of a Southern summer. Most of the people who still lived here were too old to move away. Or too settled, too scared or too shiftless to bother.

They hid in their little burrows, behind the bravado of unlocked doors and friendly smiles, because the big, bad world beyond the mountain hollow was scarier than anything they could find here.

At least, that's what they used to think.

Until he'd come.

The house on Vesper Road was small and neat, painted a pale grayish-blue with merry yellow trim. Behind the house, moonlight silhouetted Smoky Ridge, edges softened *by the lush summer growth that gave the mountain the appearance of blue velvet in the daylight.*

This house, he thought, would be locked. She'd know better than to pretend the world around her was a safe place.

But she was worth the challenge.

No one else was stirring at this time of night, no traffic moving along the two-lane road winding along the twists and turns of Bitterwood Creek. Ten miles west of Bitterwood, I-75 made it easy for travelers to bypass the town altogether on their way to the Smoky Mountain tourist traps.

Her door was locked, just as he'd expected. He tried the window by the front door and found it had been latched, as well.

Circling the house in silence, he came to a side window that looked in on her study. She was there, he saw with surprise. Her head on the desk, cheek plastered to the pages inside an open file folder. Working late, he thought with a secret smile.

Trying to catch him.

She wasn't pretty, exactly, but that had never been one of his criteria. He'd taken old women and young girls, fat and skinny, fit and fragile. Not all here in Bitterwood, of course.

Here, he'd taken only three.

He tried the latch on the window and found it open. But he couldn't get into the house this way, not with her napping so near. A loaded pistol lay on the desk beside her. One creak of the window and she'd awaken, pull the weapon and have him in her crosshairs.

He never used a gun himself if he could avoid it. It seemed too easy. Too impersonal. Snipers shot at targets from hundreds of yards away, their only connection with the soon-to-be-dead a brief, magnified view through a sniper's scope. Where was the value in such a death?

He liked to feel the heat of his victims as they struggled to hang on to their fleeting lives. Smell the iron tang of blood and hear the sounds of life leaving a body. It was intimate. The most intimate, thrilling thing he'd ever done in his whole life. Nothing else came close.

He wondered if she'd left another window open....

Ivy Hawkins woke with a start, sitting up straight in her chair. A piece of paper clung to her cheek before dropping back to the desk atop the others lying inside the open manila folder. Her gaze went automatically to the window as if she expected to see someone there.

She rubbed her tired eyes, trying to hold on to the fleeting remnants of the nightmare that had awakened her. For a moment, she had a memory of looking through her own window at herself and feeling…what?

Anticipation, she realized, feeling queasy. But when she tried to remember more about the dream, it eluded her grasp, slippery and ephemeral, leaving behind only the sour taste of fear.

She pushed to her feet and crossed to the window, sliding her hand across the latch to make sure it was in place. Her heart skipped a beat as she realized it was unlocked.

How had she left a window unlocked?

He knows it's unlocked.

Chill bumps rising on her arms and back, she quickly snapped the latch into place. And because if one window could be unlocked, so could others, she grabbed her Smith & Wesson M&P357 and went around the small farmhouse, room by room, to check the rest of the locks, as well.

Everything else was secure. She holstered the pistol and went back to the study, where she'd left her files.

Crime scene photos lay scattered across the open file, as if in death the three murder victims would share the secrets of their last moments in life. But they were mute, the bloodless marks on their carefully cleaned bodies serving as their final statements.

"You don't even know if they're connected." The impatient tone of her supervisor, Captain Rayburn, rang in her head.

He refused to admit there was a link between the deaths at all, despite the obvious evidence. Ivy suspected the captain resisted the idea because he didn't want to invite outside agencies into Bitterwood to observe the department in any way.

She had a few theories why that might be so, none of them good.

On paper, the victims *were* different enough to confuse matters—a quiet, single woman in her early thirties, a young widow with a drinking problem and a college coed home alone while her parents were visiting friends in nearby Maryville. But it was what the victims shared in common that convinced Ivy of a link.

Home alone. Living on secluded roads that saw little traffic after seven in the evening. All three murders taking place at night, between ten and midnight. And all three victims stabbed to death by a killer who had left no actionable evidence behind—because he didn't kill them in their homes. Apparently, he took them elsewhere for the kills, washed them clean of all blood and evidence and returned them to their beds to be found by concerned neighbors and loved ones.

Ivy slumped in her chair and closed the folder, a glance at her watch reminding her that she'd stayed up well past two in the morning yet again. If she went to bed right now, she'd get maybe two hours of sleep before her alarm clock rang and she'd have to start all over again. Ten days straight. That's how long it had been since she'd had a full night's sleep.

The phone on the desk rang, shattering the silence and rattling her nerves. The caller ID read "Bitterwood P.D."

She grabbed the receiver. "Hawkins."

The voice on the other line was Detective Antoine Parsons, the whipcord-lean veteran who'd been working the murders with her. What he said sent another chill skittering through her.

"We have another one."

Sutton Calhoun edged his way around the small cluster of neighbors gathered outside the farmhouse on Blalock Road, trying not to draw attention from the police officers busy at work taping off the scene and keeping people from going any farther onto the property. He kept his baseball cap low over his brow, shielding his face from any curious eyes. Fourteen years away wasn't nearly long enough for anyone around these parts to forget a Calhoun. And for the moment, at least, he'd prefer to fly under the radar.

The front door of the farmhouse opened and a tall, lean black man emerged, looking grim and angry. Sutton recognized his old friend Antoine Parsons, who hadn't changed much since their high school days. Like Sutton, Antoine had known the victim, Marjorie Kenner.

Mrs. Kenner had been the librarian at Bitterwood High School since Sutton's early high school years, a widow who'd never married again after her soldier husband's death in the Panama conflict. Sutton wondered who'd found her body at this time of night. The call he'd picked up on his police scanner hadn't specified who'd phoned 911. As far as Sutton knew, Marjorie Kenner still lived alone in the same house where she'd lived as long as he'd known her. No children, no lovers, no renters to help pay the bills.

Of course, things might have changed in the past fourteen years. He hadn't exactly kept up with the folks back home in Bitterwood once he'd got out for good. She might have met someone new, someone she shouldn't have trusted. Hell, maybe the older she'd gotten, the more she'd felt the full weight of time passing and had taken to driving into Maryville or even Knoxville for a little male companionship.

It would certainly simplify Sutton's life if Mrs. Kenner's murder had an uncomplicated explanation.

"Sutton Calhoun?" At the sound of his name, Sutton looked up and saw Antoine Parsons's dark eyes wide with surprise.

He tipped the brim of his cap up and nodded at his old friend. "How's life treatin' you, Antoine?"

Antoine's lips curved in the faintest of smiles. "Better than I deserve. Never thought I'd see you around these parts again."

"Neither did I," Sutton admitted.

The front door opened again, and a dark-haired woman emerged from the house, her gaze sweeping the yard until it settled on Antoine Parsons. Suddenly her gaze snapped back again, locking with Sutton's. Her forehead creased and she walked slowly down the front steps toward them.

Sutton's gut tightened as if he'd just taken a blow to the solar plexus. Her hair was gathered back in a tight ponytail, revealing the familiar curves and planes of her small oval face. She hadn't grown much taller than she'd been at fifteen, though even the loose-fitting blue Bitterwood P.D. golf shirt couldn't hide the fact that she'd filled out in all the right places.

"Sutton Calhoun." Her accent was as broad as the mountains surrounding them, but he couldn't tell by her tone whether she was glad to see him or dismayed. Whatever she was thinking lay hidden in the depths of her dark brown eyes.

Her lips curved without much humor. "You don't remember me, do you?"

Oh, I remember you, he thought. "Ivy Hawkins. You used to live down the road."

And you damned near saved my sanity.

She'd been a few years younger than he was, not even old enough to drive by the time he left home to join the army. But she'd been his sounding board. His secret confidante, wiser than her young years should have allowed. She'd been there when he'd broken away from his father's influence, and he'd helped her cope with her mother's revolving-door string of boyfriends.

She'd be in her late twenties now. She looked younger, maybe because she didn't have on a stitch of makeup. He noted the detective's shield on her belt. "And you're a detective."

Her dark eyes narrowed. "What are you doing here?" Her tone wasn't exactly friendly. Of course, the last time he'd seen her, she'd been crying, begging him not to leave her there alone.

He'd hoped she'd get out. Clearly she hadn't.

"Just in town for a visit," he answered.

"No, I mean here. At my crime scene."

"Oh." He wondered how much he should tell her. "I have a police scanner and heard the crime called in." That much was the truth.

"Just happened to have a police scanner?" She sounded skeptical.

"It's a hobby."

"You know those Calhouns," Antoine said lightly. "They like to know where the cops are at all times."

Sutton made a face at his old friend. *You're not helping,* he thought.

"You're up awfully late." She arched one dark eyebrow.

"Yeah." He nodded toward the house. "How bad is it?"

"Bad enough." She pulled Antoine aside, lowering her voice. But not so low that he couldn't hear what she said. "Let's call in the Violent Crime Response Team. You know our techs aren't trained to handle evidence retrieval at this level."

Antoine grimaced. "What evidence?"

"My point exactly," Ivy said flatly.

"Rayburn won't like it," Parsons warned.

Rayburn. Sutton searched his memory until he came up with a face to go with the name. Glen Rayburn had nabbed Sutton's father, Cleve, at least once. Been a real bastard about it, as Sutton recalled. Not that the old man hadn't deserved to be busted, but Rayburn had more or less told Sutton he'd be coming for him, too.

All Calhouns ended up in the cages sooner or later, he'd said.

Sutton had been smart enough to get out before he fell into his con man father's undertow. He hadn't had money for college, so he'd signed up with the U.S. Army and spent the next few years climbing the ladder through hard work and sheer cussedness.

That's how he'd ended up at Cooper Security, working for Jesse Cooper and his trouble-magnet family. The head of Cooper Security had been looking to add people with Special Forces training to his staff. Sutton had fit the bill.

Parsons moved away from Ivy, pulling out his cell phone. She turned back to Sutton, cocking her head as she saw him watching her. She closed the distance between them with deliberate steps. "I thought you swore you'd never let the dust of Bitterwood touch your feet again."

"That's a little melodramatic."

She shrugged. "You said it, not me."

True, he *had* said it. And meant it. And if Stephen Billings hadn't walked into Cooper Security two weeks ago looking for help investigating his sister's murder, he probably would've kept that vow without another thought.

He'd told himself there was nothing back in Bitterwood to tempt him to return. He'd let himself forget Ivy and her loyal, uncomplicated friendship.

Too late now. Whatever connection they'd shared fourteen years ago was clearly dead and gone, if her cool gaze meant anything.

"I'm here on a job." He kept it vague.

"What kind of job?"

Should have known vague wouldn't work with a little bulldog like Ivy Hawkins. She'd never been one to take no for an answer. "An investigation."

Her look of disbelief stung a little. "Someone hired you to investigate something here in little bitty Bitterwood?"

It did sound stupid, he had to admit. What ever happened in Bitterwood that interested anyone outside the city limits?

Maybe the truth was his best option. After all, she was technically an old friend, even if they were no longer close. And he might need all the help he could get to figure out who'd killed April Billings.

"I'm here to look into a murder that happened in Bitterwood a little over a month ago."

"April Billings," she said immediately.

He nodded. "Were you on that case?"

She shook her head. "She was the first."

Something about her tone tweaked his curiosity. "The first?"

"Murder," she said faintly. "First stranger murder in Bitterwood in twenty years."

"And you're sure it was a stranger murder?"

Her eyes met his, sharp and cautious. "All the signs were there."

"I thought you didn't investigate it."

"I didn't investigate it at the time it happened."

"But you've looked into her death since?"

She cocked her head slightly. "Who sent you to investigate this case? Are you with the TBI?"

He almost laughed at that thought. His father had had enough run-ins with the Tennessee Bureau of Investigation that both their faces were probably plastered to the Knoxville field office's front wall, right there with all the other most wanted. "No. Private investigation."

"You're a P.I.?" Her eyebrows arched over skeptical eyes.

"Sort of."

Antoine Parsons returned, saving him from having to go into any more detail. "TBI's sending their Violent Crime Response Team as soon as they can gear up and get on the road."

"Good." Ivy's gaze didn't leave Sutton's face.

She was making him feel like a suspect. He didn't like it one bit.

"Hawk, why don't you go on home now?" Parsons suggested. "I'll wait here for the TBI team and make sure our guys don't make a mess. Get some sleep and we'll hit the streets in the morning, see if we can find out why someone would kill Marjorie Kenner in her own home."

In her own home, Sutton thought. Just like April Billings. Had there been a connection between April and Marjorie? He supposed they'd been acquainted, at least in passing. At twenty, April wasn't far out of high school, and her brother had told Sutton that his sister had been a Bitterwood High School graduate, though she and her parents hadn't moved to Bitterwood until she was a freshman in high school.

Her parents had gone to Maryville with two other couples for dinner and a movie. They'd returned shortly after midnight to find their daughter dead in her bedroom upstairs. Multiple stab wounds washed clean and free of blood. The cotton pajamas in which her killer had dressed her had barely had a drop of blood on them.

"We have potential witnesses to interview." Ivy's chin came up, even though she looked bone tired. Sutton wondered if she'd been awake when the call came in about Marjorie Kenner. Pulling an all-nighter with her case files?

He'd been pulling an all-nighter himself, which was why he'd been awake to hear the dispatcher send out a call for units to respond to a 187—a homicide.

"I'll make myself scarce," Sutton told Parsons. "Leave you two to your interviews."

Ivy's hand closed over his arm as he started to walk away, her grip strong. He looked down at her hand where it circled his arm, surprised by a sudden spark of sexual awareness. Her hand was warm and dry, her touch firm, but running through his head like a motion picture were images of her hands on his body, exploring with the same sure, firm touch.

Where the hell had that reaction come from? He and Ivy had never shared that kind of connection back in the day.

Of course, back then, she'd been a skinny fifteen-year-old with sad eyes and a whole lot of pain on her plate, and he'd been a restless eighteen-year-old with one foot already out of town.

"Where are you staying, in case I need to get in touch?" Despite the casual tone she used, Sutton knew he'd be hearing from her sooner or later.

He tried not to let his suddenly fevered brain continue down the sexually charged path onto which it had already wandered. "The motel on Route 4. Stay and Save."

Her eyes widened slightly. "I see. Does Cleve know you're in town?"

"No. And I'd just as soon keep it that way." He didn't know if he could get away with being in town without running into the old man, but he sure as hell intended to try.

"You have a cell phone?"

She wasn't going to let it go, was she? He pulled a card from his pocket and handed it to her. "Nice to see you again, Ivy Hawkins."

Her eyes darkening, she took the card and stuck it in the pocket of her jeans. "Same here." He didn't think she meant it.

She held his gaze a moment longer, reigniting the flood of titillating mental images running through his brain. Then she turned and walked away without a further good-bye.

He took several deep breaths as he walked back to his Ford Ranger, trying to drag his mind back to the questions raised by the latest murder. He'd come to Bitterwood thinking he'd know pretty quickly whether or not he could help solve the Billings girl's murder.

He hadn't expected to hear about similar murders. But research had led him to two other murders in Bitterwood over the past couple of months. Three, counting Marjorie Kenner's. So, maybe not a crime of passion, as he'd suspected of April Billings's murder.

Back in the truck, he checked his email, though it was too early for anyone from the office to have come through with the information he'd requested. But apparently one of his fellow Cooper Security agents was an early riser; he had an email from Delilah Hammond waiting in his in-box.

"Call me," it said.

Uh-oh.

He dialed her number, unsurprised when she answered on the first ring. Nor was he surprised that she didn't even bother with a greeting.

"Have you lost your damned mind?"

"Hello to you, too," he said, stifling a grin.

"You had the good sense to get out of Bitterwood years ago, and you take the first job out of that godforsaken hollow that comes slithering through the office?"

Delilah Hammond had lived in Bitterwood for seventeen years before she got out on a college scholarship. She'd seen her brother Seth sucked in by Cleve Calhoun's unique brand of larcenous charm and live to pay for it. Sutton didn't blame her for her reaction. But he knew what he was doing.

"It's only for a few days," he said, keeping his voice calm and soothing.

"You are not using your reasonable tone with me, Sutton Calhoun. Tell me you're not."

"I'm not," he lied.

"Yes, you are." Her annoyance came across the phone line, clear as glass. "I'm not trying to be bossy here."

"You live to be bossy, Dee. Has anything come through from your contacts on our cold-case search request?"

"Possible hit in the Bowling Green, Kentucky, area." She sighed. "Promise me you won't let Cleve suck you into something dangerous."

"I don't plan to see Cleve."

"He'll find you. He always does."

"Just because your brother was an idiot doesn't mean

I'm going to be." He wondered where Seth was now. Sutton hadn't seen him in years, not since leaving to join the army. "You never talk about Seth."

"I'm not going to now." Her voice went instantly hard.

"Heard from him lately?"

There was a long pause on her end before she spoke, her tone resigned. "Not since I left the FBI."

She'd left the FBI eight years ago. "That long?"

"I guess I ceased being any use to him when I no longer had the pull to keep him out of trouble." Delilah's tone was sharp, but Sutton had known his old friend's sister long enough to see through her shields. Seth's abandonment hurt her, even though her life had to be a hell of a lot more trouble-free with him gone.

"He's a fool."

"Yeah. Well, nothing I can do about that. But I'll keep on these cold-case requests and see if I can't come up with more for you."

"Scan the Kentucky case information and email it to me?"

"Will do." She hung up the phone without saying goodbye.

He snapped his phone shut and leaned his head back against the seat, feeling the effects of his sleepless night. Back when he was a kid, he could stay up all night, getting into one scrape after another, and barely even feel it.

But it had been a long time since he'd been a kid. At thirty-two, he was starting to feel his age and the inevitable effects of time. Inescapable, no matter how hard he worked to stay fit and active.

He had just started the truck when a loud rap on his window jerked his nervous system into red alert. He snapped his gaze toward the window, his hand already closing over the butt of his Glock 17. He relaxed his grip as he recognized Ivy Hawkins's dark eyes gazing back at him through the window. He hit the button and the window whirred down.

"You're still here," she said.

"Had to make a phone call."

She gave a brief nod, her gaze speculative. "I could use a cup of coffee. You?"

He could, but he had a feeling Ivy wanted more than just a cup of joe. "Ledbetter's?" he asked, speaking of the only decent diner in town.

Her lips quirked. "Where else?"

"I'll meet you there."

She put her hand on the door frame, her fingers brushing his shoulder. A zing of attraction tugged at his gut. "Why don't you give me a ride? You can drop me back here when we're done."

"Why do I get the feeling this isn't a simple cup of coffee between old friends?" he asked as she settled in the passenger seat.

Her dark-eyed gaze sharpened. "Because it ain't."

Chapter Two

Bitterwood sat at the edge of farm country, which meant Ledbetter's Diner opened well before dawn to accommodate the early rising farmers and their work crews. It had also become a favorite place of anyone who worked a night shift, as the coffee was always hot and strong and the prices reasonable.

Ivy and Sutton bought coffee at the counter and took the drinks to an empty booth near the back of the diner. Sutton's lips curved slightly as he sat across from her, reminding her just why she'd fallen so hard for him back when she was just a kid. When he smiled, he could take a girl's breath away.

"When we were kids, this place was *the* place to eat, remember? Everybody with two dimes to rub together came here to get Maisey Ledbetter's peach cobbler." He took a sip of coffee and made a soft sound of contentment that traveled all the way down Ivy's nervous system to make her toes tingle.

She noted her reaction with a combination of dismay and resignation. What had she expected? There'd never been a time she could remember when she hadn't been completely susceptible to Sutton Calhoun's charms.

"With homemade vanilla ice cream," she added with

a reluctant smile. "The redneck equivalent of lunch at Spago."

Sutton's laugh was tinged with surprise. "What do you know about Spago?"

"You think just because I stuck around this hick little town I can't use the internet? Or maybe even travel now and then?" She'd planned her words to come out light and teasing, but she just sounded defensive. Exactly the opposite of what she'd intended.

"Of course not."

She pasted on a smile. "I'll admit I've only been to L.A. once. And I didn't get anywhere near Spago."

"Same here." He shot her a disarming grin that made her feel as if she was about to melt into a puddle on the booth bench.

She had to get a grip. She wasn't ready to forgive Sutton Calhoun for abandoning her when she'd needed him most. And she sure as hell couldn't afford to trust him again.

"But you didn't invite me here to talk about travel or even peach cobbler, did you?" He took another long drink of coffee, meeting her gaze over the rim of the cup.

"Why did you really come back here?"

"I told you. I was hired to look into an unsolved murder."

She took a sip of coffee and swallowed, letting the pause linger before she casually asked, "Since when does Cooper Security do private investigations?"

His dark eyebrows arched. "What do you know about Cooper Security, Ivy Hawkins?"

"Top-notch risk management firm. Stellar reputation for doing the tough, scary jobs that a lot of firms would never take on. Specializes in corporate risk training and dangerous security jobs." She hid a smile at the hint of admiration in his expression. "But I've never heard of them doing any private investigation before."

"We're branching out."

"Sounds more like a step down from all that excitement."

"Depends on the case. We only take cases where we think we can make a real difference." He set his cup of coffee down, running his finger over the rim. "It was our chopper pilot's idea, actually."

"Your chopper pilot?"

"One of the company owner's cousins. His wife was murdered a long time ago. It took him over a decade to finally find her killer. Last year, he mentioned in passing that he wished he'd had the Cooper Security resources to work with back when the case hadn't been quite so cold."

"And your boss decided to open an investigations division from that one offhand remark?" She didn't hide her skepticism. It seemed like a pretty random way to make a huge corporate decision.

"I imagine Jesse had already been considering the possibility." This time, Sutton was the one who sounded defensive. She could tell that he respected his boss and the company. "J.D.'s remark probably just crystallized the whole idea for him."

"So you're here as a P.I., then. You know, it might have been nice to give the local law a heads-up."

"Might have been," he conceded with an unrepentant smile.

"But you didn't. Why not?"

He took another long sip of coffee and didn't answer right away.

Impatience clawed at her belly as she waited, until she couldn't stay quiet any longer. "You don't trust the local cops?"

His gaze snapped up to meet hers. "That's an interesting question. What made you ask it?"

"Your clear reluctance to make yourself known to the local authorities, for one thing. Maybe you think we can't be trusted."

"I didn't hide from y'all at the crime scene."

"You didn't exactly announce yourself, either."

"And that's your only reason for wondering if I don't trust the local LEOs?" He was the one who looked skeptical now.

She didn't miss his use of the acronym LEO, short for Law Enforcement Officer. He could talk the talk, it seemed. But could he walk the walk, as well? "You're the one who brought it up."

"No, all I did was agree that I probably should have made a courtesy call to the local police. You're the one who ran with the idea of that the cops can't be trusted." He leaned toward her. "Do you think it's possible a cop could be involved, Detective Hawkins?"

She didn't answer.

"How's your mama?" he asked after a few moments of silence.

"Unchanged," she answered flatly.

"Just like my dad."

She arched an eyebrow. Odd thing to say about his father, considering. "I suppose once you get in the habit of a certain way of life," she said carefully, "it's hard to make a change."

Apparently that was one thing from their shared past that had remained the same. She still had a weak-willed, naive mother who, though she recently turned sixty, was still going from man to man in search of some ill-defined, unachievable romantic bliss, leaving Ivy to clean up her messes and, one time at least, directly suffer the consequences of her bad choices. And Sutton's daddy had spent most of his adult life skating the edge of the law, somehow managing to avoid more than the occasional slap on the wrist and a day or two in the local lockup.

Of course, Cleve Calhoun hadn't been causing much trouble for anyone in the past few years....

"I came here thinking I'd be looking at just one murder." Sutton broke into her thoughts. "I don't suppose you could make my job a lot easier by telling me April Billings's murder is unrelated to the others?"

"Depends on who you ask," she said drily. "Some people around these parts think we just hit an unlucky streak."

"Four stranger murders in Bitterwood, Tennessee? In under two months?" Sutton's eyebrows rose. "One hell of an unlucky streak."

"Not everyone is convinced they *are* stranger murders." Her coffee had already started to go cold; she shoved the cup away with a grimace.

"There are people on the force who actually think these women were killed by people they know? Four different people they know?"

She shrugged. "Apparently Bitterwood is a seething hotbed of suppressed homicidal passions."

Sutton laughed softly. "Okay."

She'd figured if she ever set eyes on Sutton Calhoun again, he'd suffer in comparison to her lingering girlhood memories. Nobody could live up to that idealized image of vigorous youthful masculinity.

But damned if the grown-up version didn't come awfully close. His smoky hazel eyes had an unnerving tendency to smolder when he smiled, a reminder that he might be more honorable than his swindler father, but he was just as dangerous a charmer.

"I do think the murders are connected," she admitted. "The victimology might lead you to think otherwise—"

"Because they're different ages and had different life-styles?"

She narrowed her eyes. "How'd you learn all this information so fast?"

"Research." At her look of skepticism, he inclined his head slightly. "Someone at Cooper Security has a former army buddy who now works for the Tennessee Bureau of Investigation."

"Someone in the crime lab," she guessed.

"I honestly don't know. He just emailed me the information. I didn't ask any questions about his source."

"So you know there are plenty of similarities between the murders, even if the victims' ages and lifestyles aren't that similar."

"Crime scene similarities, sure. Late-evening times of death, the first three, at least, killed with a knife from the victim's own kitchen. But none of the murders take place in their homes. They were all killed somewhere else and returned to their homes after death. No evidence left behind." His eyes narrowed. "Which I suppose *might* raise the question of whether your perp could be a cop. Is it a theory you're seriously entertaining?"

"There are a lot of theories I'm entertaining at the moment," she admitted. "We still don't know how he gains entrance. Never any sign of a break-in. And how do you stab women to death and leave zero evidence at the scene? No excess blood, despite the bodies often being partially exsanguinated. Little sign of a struggle."

"He seems to surprise his victims when they're vulnerable," Sutton said thoughtfully. "Late at night, when most people are in bed. These women were all attacked when they were asleep, I'd bet."

For a second, an image flitted through her mind. She saw herself, head down on the desk in her study, dead asleep. It was as if she were looking at herself through someone else's eyes. She tamped down a hard shudder.

"Is something wrong?" Sutton asked.

She shook her head. "No. And yes, we believe they were attacked when they were asleep. Clearly he takes them and kills them somewhere else—explaining the lack of blood and other evidence where the bodies are found. Then he returns them to their beds. That's a crazy way to kill people, but that looks to be how all four murders happened. What are the odds they're unrelated?"

"Nonexistent."

Well, damn, she thought, her heart sinking. *I've just spilled my guts about a serial murder spree to a civilian just because he's sexy and I'm weak. What the hell have I done?*

As if reading her mind, Sutton leaned toward her, laying his hand on top of hers on the table. "You know I'm not going to use anything you told me in any way that would hurt your case."

Her skin seemed to burn where he touched her. She pulled her hand away. "Make damned sure you don't. And if you find anything I need to know, you'll call me. Right?"

"Call you at the police station?"

She almost flinched at the thought. The last thing she needed was a call from Sutton Calhoun coming through the department phone system. Might as well put a sign on her back—stupid girl detective can't keep her mouth shut *or* solve a case without outside help. "Cell phone," she said, pulling her business card from her wallet and pushing it across the table to him.

He sat back and studied the card for a moment, his expression thoughtful. "I never would have figured you for the detective type, back in the day. I thought you'd be a teacher or something. But now that I think of it, the clues were all there. You were always a curious little thing. Always saw a mystery in everything. Remember that time you thought old Mr. Valery had killed his wife because you hadn't seen her in days?"

She smiled. "Well, I was right that she was missing. How was I supposed to know she'd had a fight with him and gone to stay with her mother for a few days?"

He grinned. "Good thing I talked you out of calling the police."

"You just didn't trust the police in general."

His smile faded. "Yeah, we Calhouns didn't exactly have any friends in blue. You never called the police if you could avoid it."

"And here you are a private eye."

"And you're a detective." He cocked his head, his hazel eyes narrowing. "Aren't you a little young to be a detective? You're what, twenty-eight? Twenty-nine?"

"Twenty-nine. I'm pretty sure I made detective so quickly because the force didn't have a female investigator."

"Trying to meet a quota?"

"Something like that."

"Well, it worked out this time, for both of you." His smile looked genuine, but Calhouns were notorious for their easy deceit. "You're working a job you're obviously good at, and the force benefits from a good detective who also gives them a box to mark on their diversity checklist."

"No need to feed me a line of bull, Calhoun. I don't have the clout to get you in on this investigation. Or keep you out."

One dark eyebrow lifted, but he didn't comment. A

tense silence continued between them after that, until she broke it by suggesting they head back to the crime scene.

Once they were belted into the truck, Ivy asked, "How long have you been with Cooper Security?"

"Two years."

"What did you do the other twelve years? How long did you stay in the army?"

"All twelve years. I went straight to Cooper Security from the army. One of the boss's brothers-in-law knew me from there, and I was ready for a change of pace."

"Change of pace? From one dangerous job to another?"

"Slight change of pace." He nodded in concession.

"So, an army buddy vouched for you? I'd assumed Delilah Hammond must have gotten you an interview or something."

"I don't think Delilah has many kind thoughts about anyone or anything from Bitterwood," he said with a wry smile.

"No, I don't suppose she would." She and Delilah hadn't been best friends or anything, but she ran into Delilah's mother occasionally, usually on a drunk and disorderly call. Once she sobered up, she was a typical proud mother, telling all the cops at the jail about her daughter, the former FBI agent who was working for a big international security firm.

"I hear some amazing things about your company," she added as they headed back toward the crime scene. Dawn had broken while they were at the diner, and the sun was creeping closer and closer to the mountaintop horizon. "Y'all took down the president's chief of staff last year, right? For corruption and conspiracy to commit murder?"

"I wasn't directly involved with that." His tone was careful, and she supposed she might be treading on classified territory with her questions.

"Delilah was, though. At least, that's what her mother claims." She smiled wryly. "I'm sure she'd be horrified to know Reesa brags about her from the drunk tank. I remember how she felt about her mother's drinking."

"Do you ever see Seth Hammond?" Sutton sounded curious.

"Now and then. He moves around a lot. Last I heard, he was living in Maryville. Or maybe it was Knoxville." She grimaced. "He's already shafted just about everyone here in Bitterwood. I guess he had to find somewhere new to run his cons."

"So he's still doing that, then." Sutton sounded disappointed. He'd been friends with Seth as a kid, she remembered suddenly. She hadn't thought of them together in a long time. As they'd both grown older, Seth Hammond's fascination with Sutton's father's lifestyle, and Sutton's growing disgust with it, had pushed the two friends far apart.

And pushed Sutton closer to her. For a while, at least.

"I guess he still is. I don't know if he knows how to do anything else," she said. "He didn't exactly have the best role models growing up."

Sutton grimaced. "That's no excuse. His sister Delilah turned out just fine, and she came from the same family."

"You turned out pretty well, too, considering."

He slanted a thoughtful look at her. "Maybe. I suppose none of us really got out of here unscathed."

She certainly hadn't, she thought bleakly. Life with her undependable, often foolish mother had taken a heavy toll on her chances at a normal life. By the age of sixteen, she'd no longer had any illusions about romance, love or sex. She'd seen too much, suffered too much to think of romantic love as anything pure or uplifting.

She'd had boyfriends. She'd had sex. But she'd never

had that elusive thing called love that her mother seemed desperate to find, and she had no intentions of ever looking for it.

Back at Marjorie Kenner's house, most of the onlookers had dispersed, leaving only police cars and a vehicle marked with the TBI's insignia. "That was fast," she said, nodding toward the new arrival.

Sutton pulled up next to Antoine Parsons's Ford Focus and looked toward the front door. "Your boss is here."

She followed Sutton's gaze and spotted her supervisor, Captain Rayburn, standing in the doorway talking to Parsons.

Well, hell.

INCOMPETENCE WAS BAD enough, Sutton thought as he and Ivy headed up the front walk, but in Glen Rayburn's case, he'd never been sure whether the captain was merely inept at his job or actively corrupt.

He'd made it to captain the way a lot of cops in a lot of small towns did—by making friends with the mayor and city council. He did favors for anyone in the department above him, often at his own expense, and got away with being a careless, corner-cutting cop as a result.

Rayburn's eyes narrowed to slits as he recognized Sutton. He didn't bother with politeness. "What the hell are you doing here?"

"I have family in town," Sutton answered airily.

"You ain't got no family here at my crime scene."

Your crime scene? Sutton forced himself not to look at Ivy for her reaction, aware that it might turn Rayburn's displeasure toward the detective instead of Sutton himself.

But Rayburn apparently had plenty of displeasure to go around, for he turned his baleful gaze on Ivy and asked, "You brought him here, Hawkins?"

"I came here on my own," Sutton answered before Ivy could speak. "Matter of fact, Detective Hawkins just gave me the third degree—why was I here, what do I want, how long am I going to be in town—"

"And?"

"He's been hired by one of the victims' brothers," Ivy answered. "To look into her murder."

Rayburn turned his attention back to Sutton. "Somebody hired you?"

"Yes."

"Mind if I ask who?"

Stephen Billings hadn't asked him to keep his identity a secret, and Sutton had already told Ivy who his client was. Still, he gave Rayburn's question a moment of thought before he answered, wondering if there was any way Rayburn could use Billings's identity against him. "April Billings's brother," he answered finally.

"April Billings's murder has nothing to do with this crime scene," Rayburn said firmly. He sounded as if he believed it.

Was he really that self-delusional? Or was he desperate to believe there were no connected murders in Bitterwood because the alternative might bring state and federal investigators swooping down on the small mountain town, putting all the police department's secrets under a bright light of scrutiny?

"Maybe not," he said aloud, trying to keep his tone friendly. "I just wanted to talk to the detectives on the case, see what territory's already been covered so I'll know where to start."

"That's not going to happen again." His face darkening with anger, Rayburn shot Ivy a warning look. "Understand?"

"Yes, sir." Her voice was tight with annoyance, but if Rayburn noticed, he didn't comment.

Instead, he turned back to Sutton. "Leave my detectives out of your investigation. That's not what we pay them to do."

Swallowing a smart-mouthed retort, Sutton nodded and turned away, walking slowly to his truck.

He spared a glance back at the crime scene as he cranked the truck and put it into gear. Rayburn had already moved on, talking to the TBI agents milling near the state agency's van. But Ivy Hawkins's gaze was still turned his way, the look on her face thoughtful.

He felt a flare of regret at the realization that she was now officially off-limits to him, regret that had nothing to do with what she could offer him as a detective in charge of the case he'd been hired to investigate.

Instead, it had everything to do with the way his libido had gone on high alert the second she'd walked out of Marjorie Kenner's front door—and his memories of her friendship came roaring back as well, reminding him that she'd once been his lifeline.

He passed his father's ramshackle old house on the way back to the motel, and for a moment, he considered stopping in to see how the old man was faring. He hadn't seen him since he'd left town, hadn't talked to him in nearly as many years, and the handful of Bitterwood natives he'd run into over the years had been in no hurry to bring up the unpleasant topic of his father, to his relief.

He drove on without slowing down. Some parts of his past he had no intention of revisiting.

The clerk who ran the Stay and Save Motel's front office called his name as he walked past, drawing him inside the small sandstone building. "Somebody left a message for you," he said, holding out a half-crumpled piece of paper.

He gave Sutton an expectant look as he handed over the message.

"Thanks." Sutton pulled a couple of dollars from his wallet and handed it to the clerk. He unfolded the message as he walked down the covered walkway to his room.

The message was short and sweet. "Clingmans Dome observation tower, 7 p.m. Come alone."

Chapter Three

Clearly, sleep deprivation had taken a toll on her normal good sense, because there was no logical explanation why she had bypassed the turnoff to her house on Vesper Road and continued down the two-lane highway to the Stay and Save Motel on Route 4. After fifteen straight hours on the job, she'd finally taken Antoine's advice and clocked out just after five-thirty so she could head home to catch up on some sleep.

Instead, she was at the far end of the Stay and Save parking lot, scanning for any sign of Sutton Calhoun's truck and kicking herself for being such a reckless idiot.

Rayburn had told her not to contact Sutton. Yet here she was, the second she slipped the captain's line of sight, defying his order. And for what? Sutton Calhoun might be sexy as hell and still chock-full of masculine mystery, but she hadn't gotten any sense, during their conversation early that morning, that he knew anything more about the murders than she knew herself. And that should be the only thing about Sutton Calhoun that held any interest for her now.

She didn't see Sutton's truck parked in the guest lot. At this time of the evening, he was probably out to dinner somewhere. Maybe catching up with old friends who still lived in the area. His old girlfriend Carla was still in Bitterwood, recently divorced and nearly as pretty as she'd been years earlier, when she'd been the homecoming queen who'd defied her parents to date a mysterious bad boy from the wrong side of the tracks.

Her cell phone rang, giving her tired nervous system a jolt. She checked the display and sighed, thumbing the answer button. "Hi, Mom."

"I guess you're not coming for dinner?"

Damn. "I picked up a new case. I'm sorry. Rain check?"

"Of course." Her mother, Arlene, had perfected the art of passive-aggressive accommodation. "I can freeze the pot roast for next time."

Ivy laid her head back against the headrest, feeling a vein throbbing hard in her temple. "You know you should always call me before you go to the trouble of cooking anything, Mom. My schedule is crazy."

"I know, Birdy." Ivy stifled a smile at the old nickname her mother still used for her. "I just need to talk to you soon."

"Absolutely. I'll call you as soon as things slow down." Although, she reminded herself with no small measure of guilt, there wasn't any reason she shouldn't head over to her mother's now instead of sitting here stalking Sutton Calhoun.

Ivy pressed her fingers against her gritty eyes. *Go to your mother's house, Hawkins. Just put your car in gear and go before you embarrass yourself any further.*

"Mom, listen." She had already reached for the ignition key when she saw a dark gray Ford Ranger sweep by the parking lot entrance, heading east. The truck looked a lot like Sutton's Ford, though in the waning evening light, she couldn't get a good look at the driver through the tinted windows. As it moved past, she spotted the Alabama tag on the rear bumper.

Before she thought better of it, she started her Jeep and pulled out onto the road behind him. "Mom, I've got to go. Something's just come up. I'll call you tomorrow and we can reschedule, okay?"

She hung up her phone and followed the Ranger east.

WHOEVER WAS DRIVING the black Jeep Wrangler behind Sutton was pretty good at tailing. If he weren't already on high alert and well trained, Sutton might not have spotted the vehicle keeping track of him. He'd noticed the Jeep as he entered the Smoky Mountains National Park. It stayed a couple of vehicles behind him, never getting too close. But the Jeep never let him get too far ahead, either.

Hell, maybe he ought to just pull off at the next scenic overlook and see what happened.

A glance at the truck's dashboard clock killed that idea. He was already cutting it close. Clingmans Dome was over an hour's drive from Bitterwood, and if the gathering clouds lowering over the mountains were anything to go by, a storm was brewing. Rain would slow him down. And even if he arrived with time to spare, there was the climb to the observation deck, possibly in the pouring rain.

The fifty-four-foot-tall concrete tower ending in a saucer-shaped deck stood at the summit of Tennessee's highest elevation. To get there, a visitor generally made a steep half-mile trek up a paved road. Sutton had hiked that road more than once during his boyhood, usually as part of a class trip or as the guest of another boy whose father, unlike Cleve Calhoun, wasn't allergic to a little exertion.

He hadn't been there in years, but he found the twisting mountain roads leading to the Clingmans Dome Trail familiar. The mountain straddled the state line between Tennessee and North Carolina, right in the heart of the Smoky Mountains. Some of the roads seemed to fold in on themselves as they tunneled through the mountains and curved around rocky outcroppings, making for a hair-raising drive.

Why Clingmans Dome? he wondered yet again as he kept one eye on the winding road and the other on the Jeep behind him. Why tonight at seven, with the setting sun being quickly swallowed by dark rain clouds and temperatures dropping to twenty degrees colder than in the valleys below?

He'd known, as a native of these hills, to bring warm, weather-resistant clothes, for even in the summer, evenings in the Smoky Mountains could be uncomfortably cool and wet. Up on Clingmans Dome, over a mile above sea level, the temperature could dip near freezing on an early September night, and the whole area was a coniferous rain forest, which meant getting wet was always a strong possibility.

It was an odd spot for a mysterious rendezvous, and his decision to comply with the note hadn't been made lightly. Following protocol, he'd called Jesse Cooper to tell him about the mysterious message. Cooper had wanted to send backup, but Sutton had talked his boss out of the idea. The note had said to come alone, and if his combination of Special Forces training and Cooper Security refreshers had prepared him for anything, it was to face dangers on his own if necessary.

Of course, if the Jeep trailing doggedly behind him kept up the tail, he wouldn't be going alone after all.

He knew it was possible, perhaps even likely, that he was driving toward an ambush. He'd prepared for that possibility, from wearing a GPS tracker that Jesse Cooper was even now monitoring from his office in Maybridge, Alabama, to strapping on an extra pistol—a SIG Sauer P238 in an ankle holster on his right leg in addition to his Glock, currently nestled snugly in a holster under his leather jacket.

And there were other ways to hike to the top of Clingmans Dome besides the tourist trail.

SOMEWHERE SOUTHEAST OF Gatlinburg, heading east on Highway 441, Ivy made a rookie mistake. She let an 18-wheeler pass her on a downhill straightaway and ended up stuck behind the behemoth as it groaned its way up a steep grade, putting her farther and farther behind Sutton's Ford Ranger. By the time they came across another safe area to pass and she whipped the Jeep around the lumbering truck, she'd lost sight of Sutton's vehicle completely.

"Damn it!" she growled, banging her hand on the steering wheel in frustration. Her decision to follow Sutton this far out of Bitterwood was already looking like complete idiocy, and now she'd botched even that. She was almost an hour away from home, with gritty eyes wanting to slam shut, and she was the worst cop in the world at tailing a vehicle. And piling on the bad news, there wasn't a decent turnoff for the next few miles, which meant she would have even that much farther to go before she could crawl beneath her covers for a few hours of humiliated sleep.

Around a tight curve, a side road finally came into view. Ivy flashed her right-turn indicator and eased the Jeep onto the side road. The surface of the smaller road was pocked and pitted, the ride immediately rougher. Ivy tightened her grip on the steering wheel as she slowed to pull a U-turn.

Suddenly, a pair of bright lights filled her windshield, blinding her for a moment. Startled, she jammed on her brakes, even though the lights were still some distance away. Her tires squealed in protest, the back end of the Jeep fishtailing just long enough to set her heart racing.

The lights went out again, leaving her blinded for a moment, even with the Jeep's headlights cutting through the deepening darkness. She saw a brief flash of movement, shadowy and quick. It was gone before she blinked. Swallowing hard, she turned the steering wheel hard to finish the U-turn.

And there in her headlights, impossibly close, stood Sutton Calhoun, aiming the barrel of a large black Glock right at her.

He moved toward the Jeep carefully, the barrel of the pistol staying fixed on her. She cautiously lowered the driver's side window. "Sutton, it's me. Ivy Hawkins."

He didn't lower the pistol. "Why are you following me?"

She decided the truth was the least humiliating answer. "To see where you were going."

He stopped beside her car door, gazing at her through the open window. Though his expression was stern, the corner of his mouth twitched. Her own lips curved in response. He lowered the Glock and slid it into a holster beneath his black leather jacket.

"So," she prodded when he remained silent, "where *are* you going? And why did you just pull your weapon on me?"

He released a long, slow breath and reached into the front pocket of his jeans, withdrawing a crumpled slip of paper. He handed it to her through the window and took a step back, folding his arms across his chest.

A chilling wind, damp with the promise of rain, swirled through the open window, fluttering the piece of notepaper as she clicked on the dome light to see what was written there.

"Clingmans Dome observation tower, 7 p.m. Come alone."

She read it twice, then flipped it over for any sign of a signature. There was nothing.

She turned off the dome light and looked up at Sutton. He was little more than a silhouette against a stormy, darkening sky. "Who sent this?"

"I don't know." His voice rumbled like thunder in the dark.

"You don't know?" A shiver skated down her spine. "Are you crazy, coming out here alone to meet someone who sent you an anonymous note? Haven't you ever heard of an ambush?"

She could see just enough of his face to make out a wry grin curving Sutton's lips. "You're one to talk, Ivy Hawkins, following a heavily armed man deep into the heart of the Smoky Mountains."

A flush spread over the back of her neck. "Fair enough. And you're not the only one heavily armed, by the way."

Silence fell between them, brief but tense. Sutton was the one to break it. "How'd you come to follow me, anyway?"

"I dropped by the Stay and Save to talk to you, but you weren't there. Then I saw you drive past and—"

"You decided to traipse along behind me?"

She shot him a glare. "I'm pretty sure I've never traipsed in my life."

His lips twitched again. "Didn't your boss tell you to keep clear of me?"

"Yeah, well, it's not like I sent him my itinerary."

He lifted his hand to his face. She heard the soft rasp of his palm against his beard stubble as he fell silent for a long beat. Then, just as she was searching for something else to say to break the taut silence, he dropped his hand to his side. His shoulders squared and he bent toward her, his face filling her window. He was so close, she felt his soft exhalation on her cheek, and her heart rate skittered a notch higher.

"I'm going to Clingmans Dome tonight," he said quietly. "I need to know who sent me that note and why. And I won't think any less of you if you turn around right now and head back home."

"But?"

"But I'd rather have backup as not. And since you're already here and, as you were quick to tell me, heavily armed—"

"I'll do it," she blurted, before her weariness and her native caution had time to make her think better of the idea.

He nodded, as if he had expected nothing else. "You always did have my back, didn't you?"

His words, so soft and intimate, made her shiver with a combination of pleasure and pain. Most of her memories of Sutton Calhoun seemed to be wrapped up in those two emotions.

"So, what's the plan?" she asked.

He smiled, his teeth gleaming in the dark. "How long has it been since you did a little hiking in the woods?"

BY THE TIME THEY PARKED both vehicles in the visitor lot where Clingmans Dome Road ended and the paved hiking trail to the observation deck began, a steady light rain had begun falling. Bypassing the road, they crossed into the gloomy woods, Sutton taking the lead. He slowed his pace slightly to accommodate Ivy's shorter legs, but to her credit, she kept pace without complaining, even though he could tell from the purple shadows lingering like bruises beneath her eyes that she was running on fumes.

At least she was dressed for the weather, in a weatherproof jacket and sturdy water-resistant boots. She'd lived in the mountains her whole life, too.

"You shouldn't be here," he murmured when they took a brief water break halfway to the observation deck. "You look dead on your feet."

She swallowed a swig of water. "Thanks."

"Did you get any sleep at all last night before you were called to the crime scene?"

"Some."

"What, an hour?"

She handed the water bottle back to him. "What do you expect to find at the observation deck?"

"I don't rightly know," he admitted. "An ambush, maybe."

"And yet you came alone?"

"Not my brightest idea," he conceded.

"But you couldn't let the mystery lie unsolved?" She sounded as if she understood. Hell, she probably did. She'd become a cop for some reason, after all, and it sure as hell couldn't be for the good pay, easy hours or accommodating bosses.

"These murders are connected," he said flatly.

"I know." Her serious expression was oddly endearing. She was so small, so young, so earnest. Had he ever been that earnest in his life?

"All the signs point to a serial murderer. Do you agree?"

She wiped the rain out of her eyes, not answering immediately.

"You don't agree?"

"I don't know," she said. "It's like there's something important I'm missing, but I don't yet know what it is." She looked a little sheepish. "I know that sounds stupid."

He shook his head. "No. I get it."

"I do think they're connected, though."

He nodded toward the dark mountain rising above them. "Let's get back on the trail."

GUNS WEREN'T HIS TOOL of choice. They were too impersonal. Too easy to distance oneself from a target behind the scope of a gun. And almost any person with decent eye-hand coordination could do considerable damage with a gun. Where was the fun in that? But sometimes, a high-powered rifle with a nightscope could be just the tool a man needed.

The Clingmans Dome observation deck had started clearing out around sunset as darkness and gathering storm clouds swallowed the stunning 360-degree view of the Smoky Mountains and damp night air drove out the mild warmth of the September day. He'd set the meeting deliberately after sunset, not wanting collateral damage to muddy his plan. He hadn't planned for rain, though he should have. No matter. He'd still have the advantage.

Of course, the real problem was killing Sutton Calhoun wasn't actually *his* plan. Given his own preference, he'd have chosen to let the man live. He liked a challenge, and the company Calhoun worked for was supposedly legendary, from what he'd been told.

He suspected he would have enjoyed the battle of wits with Calhoun. From what he understood about the man's past, he came from a shrewd, wily father whose native charm had parted many a man from his hard-earned money. Even if the son had taken a path more straight and narrow, he still had those instincts inside. Instincts that might make him an interesting opponent.

Seemed a shame to waste such an opportunity for sport, especially as he had an idea how he could use Calhoun's skills for his own purposes.

The observation deck remained empty, though according to his watch, seven o'clock had passed several minutes ago. So Calhoun was already living up to his reputation. He hadn't fallen for the obvious trick.

Which meant Calhoun was somewhere out there in the woods, sneaking up on the target rather than approaching it head-on. The thought that the investigator had ignored the note he'd left wasn't even an option. No man in search of answers could have resisted the opportunity presented.

He put down the binoculars and picked up the night-vision scope he'd brought along for just such a turn of events. Slowly, methodically, he started to scan the stands of spruce, hemlock and fir trees that carpeted Clingmans Dome. Water splashed the scope's lens, but not enough to eclipse the dead Fraser firs, victims of European aphids, that stood like stark white skeletons, drawing his attention momentarily away from his task. No life in them, their towering majesty reduced to brittle bones by an insect so tiny it could barely be seen at a glance.

Of course, no aphid had killed a tree alone. It took thousands to accomplish the task. That was the difference between insects and humans.

One human was capable of many wonderful, horrible things.

Movement beyond the tree husks caught his attention. Through the night-vision scope, the man moving up the mountain glowed green, an incandescent bug waiting to be squashed. But he wasn't alone. A second figure brought up the rear. Though a jacket hid the contours of her body and a baseball cap hid her features, he was sure the second person was a female.

He had built-in radar for women.

So. Two for one, then.

THE TREE BESIDE Ivy splintered, shooting shards of dead fir bark prickling against her cheek. "Ow!" she growled, lifting her hand to her face. She drew back her hand and saw the dark imprint of blood on her fingers, diluted by the rain beading on her cheeks.

"Get down!" Sutton grabbed her arm and dragged her to the ground, rolling both their bodies sideways until they were hunkered behind a small outcropping of time-worn stone. The ground was wet and loamy beneath her jeans, cold water soaking through the denim with uncomfortable speed.

"Was that—?"

"A rifle shot?" he finished for her, his voice as grim as the grave. "Yeah, it definitely was."

Great. Just great. Sutton Calhoun had led her smack-dab in the middle of trouble again, just like old times.

"Well," she said in a flat drawl, "I reckon we can officially call this an ambush."

Chapter Four

Sutton could see nothing in the gloom up the mountain, but he knew the shooter must be up there somewhere, better prepared for the conditions than he was. As he hunkered behind a large rock outcropping, he looked himself and Ivy over with the quick, practiced eye of a man used to lying low. Both of them had dressed for stealth, whether consciously or by chance. His black jeans, T-shirt and jacket blended in with the darkness so well that he could barely see his own legs.

Ivy's dark green uniform jacket nearly disappeared into the trees and underbrush around them, and her jeans were inky with rain, rendering them nearly as hard to see as his own black jeans.

"How the hell can he see us well enough to get that close with his shot?" Ivy growled, speaking aloud his own silent question.

"I think he may have a night-vision scope or something," Sutton whispered. "The darker it gets, the better he'll be able to see us."

"Do you have any idea who it could be?"

"No. But not that many people know I have a room at the Stay and Save." He risked a quick peek over the top of their rocky cover, earning another round from their hidden ambusher. The bullet shattered the sedimentary stone, forcing Sutton to duck to avoid the shrapnel.

"If he has enough ammo, he could shoot this rock to pieces," Ivy growled, brushing shards of stone out of her face.

"And if we move, he'll see us with that scope." They needed backup. But when he pulled out his phone to dare a quick check, he got an "out of range" message. "No bars."

Ivy checked her phone, as well. "Me, either." She shoved her phone back into her pocket and looked toward the direction from which the bullets had been coming. "Are you sure he's using a night-vision scope?"

"I don't think there's any other way he could shoot at us in the dark with such accuracy."

"Then we might have half a chance," she whispered, her voice taking on a hint of excitement. "Did you hear what I just heard?"

It took a second to figure out what she was talking about. Then the rumbling sound that hadn't quite registered with him earlier came again, nearer than before.

"That was thunder."

"The storm's getting closer," she murmured, hunkering down into a tighter ball.

"And with thunder comes lightning," he whispered, realizing what she was getting at. A night-vision scope was a powerful tool in the dark. But unless the person wielding the rifle out there was using a top-grade military scope, a flash of lightning, if it struck close, might be bright enough to render him temporarily blind for a few precious seconds. Maybe this night was going to turn out lucky for them after all.

"What if it doesn't work?" she asked.

"It's the only option we have." The storm was moving in quickly, the sky overhead lowering steadily. Already roiling black clouds obscured the top of Clingmans Dome, lightning sparking around the edges, too faint and far away for their purpose.

A bullet pinged against the rocky outcropping, shooting another blast of stone shards into the air around them. A sharp piece sliced across his jawline and he bit back a grunt of pain. That time, he'd heard the muted report of the rifle, dampened by whatever sound suppressor their assailant was using. Was he getting closer?

Electricity crackled in the air for a split second before the mountain lit up as bright as a high school football field on a Tennessee Friday night. Simultaneously, a deafening thunderclap crashed, echoing through the hills.

"Now!" Sutton grabbed Ivy's hand and pulled her to her feet, starting a reckless zigzag down the treacherous, rain-slick trail, his feet tangling in fallen limbs and underbrush. Ivy stumbled as she hit a slippery spot, and he grabbed her to keep her from pitching down a sharp incline.

The rifle fire didn't come right away, but when it came, it whistled so close to Sutton's ear he swore he felt the blast of air on his cheek. Whatever advantage the lightning flash had offered was gone, and he dived for cover behind a nearby Fraser fir, hoping the young tree's wide limbs and thick foliage would offer enough cover until the next lightning flash.

Thunder rumbled down the mountain, a promise of more lightning strikes to come. But would another big one happen soon enough to prevent the shooter from getting so close he couldn't miss?

"I can't tell if he's a bad shot or a good one," Ivy whispered, her breathing harsh and fast.

"Good, I think," Sutton answered. "He's having to compensate for the sound suppressor and the distance, but he's getting damned close."

"How far away?"

"No more than two hundred yards by now, I'd guess." He checked his cell phone again. Still no bars. "You got a signal?"

She checked quickly. "Nope."

He muttered a curse. "Any chance a park service employee will hear the gunfire?"

"Not sound-suppressed that way, and not over the thunder." Her tone was bleak.

Lightning illuminated the mountain again, bright as daylight. This time, Ivy needed no urging. She was already on the run before the thunder crashed, leaving Sutton to keep up with her short, churning legs.

No rifle fire answered the thunder this time, only more lightning and more crashing booms. They kept running, the harsh sound of their respiration overtaking even the roar of the downpour. Despite the breakneck pace, to Sutton the flight down the mountain seemed to take hours. But when he glanced at his watch as his feet hit the pavement of the parking lot, he saw that little more than an hour and a half had passed since he and Ivy left the parking lot and headed into the woods.

Their vehicles were the only ones left in the parking lot, offering scant cover if the gunman followed them the rest of the way down the mountain. Ivy hurried to her Jeep, putting it between her and the gunman. Since it was closer than his truck, Sutton hunkered down beside her, bending close.

"I think he may have headed back up the mountain."

"Just because he stopped shooting?" Her breathing was already returning to normal, a sign of just what good shape she was in. At some point during the day, she'd changed out of the Bitterwood P.D. polo shirt into a dark blue blouse, now visible under her open jacket, revealing a slim and

muscular physique beneath her womanly curves. Her toned
legs, outlined by the clinging wet denim, were damn near
breathtaking.

No time for horn dogging, Calhoun.

As if the heavens themselves thought he needed a reminder, lightning split the air with a deafening boom,
prickles of electricity raising the hair all over his body.
Beside him, Ivy's body gave a jerk, and for a second, he
was afraid she'd been struck. But she scrambled to her feet
and unlocked the Jeep door in one fluid movement, diving
into the front seat. She reached across, fumbling with the
lock on the passenger door until it disengaged. She shoved
the door open. "Get in!"

He complied, closing out the rain and the sparking
flashes of lightning surrounding them like an electrical
cage. In the driver's seat, Ivy was breathing hard and trembling, but she was also laughing.

He stared at her with alarm, wondering if the past few
minutes of sheer terror had sent her off the deep end. His
expression only made her laugh harder.

"My mama always told me you were nothin' but trouble," she drawled, still laughing. "I don't think this is what
she meant, though."

Damn, he wanted to reach across the seat and kiss that
grin off her soft pink lips, the urge so strong it felt like another jolt to his system. Why her? Why now? Was it just
the heightened danger? Her sheer proximity?

He'd been in dangerous situations before. Worked side
by side with beautiful women, but he'd never felt this up-
ended before, and by little Ivy Hawkins, of all people. He'd
been about as close to her as he'd been to anyone, all those
years ago, but never once had he been tempted to kiss her.

But she's all grown up now, Calhoun. Sexy in that natural, thoughtless way of some Southern girls, who could

make a man's blood sing just by flashing a toothy grin. Or smelling like morning sunshine even when drenched and shivering.

He forced his straying mind back to their still-dangerous situation before his unexpected lust got them killed. "I reckon we should call in the local LEOs. Agreed?"

She nodded. "I know a Sevier County deputy." She checked her phone, her grin telling him she'd finally gotten a signal—and making his insides tighten into a hot, hungry knot. She made a quick call to someone named John, giving their location. "He's still out there, John. I don't know if we're safe yet."

The Jeep wouldn't offer much cover if their mystery shooter decided to send a few more rounds of lead their way. Too many windows. But Sutton's truck wouldn't be much better, and getting out of the vehicle while a lightning storm raged around them would be pretty stupid.

"This doesn't make any sense," Ivy growled after she hung up the phone, wiping rainwater away from her face. A little scratch on her cheek was trickling blood, but not a lot. She probably wouldn't even need a bandage, he noted with relief. They'd been lucky. It could have been so much worse. "Does this ambush even have anything to do with the murders? What the hell was the point of luring you out here and gunning you down?"

"I don't know," he admitted. "Your perp hasn't used a gun in any of the murders so far, right?"

"Right. Just knives and ligatures. Ligatures to control, knives to dispatch." Her trembling had eased to almost nothing. Talking shop seemed to have put her back in control of her nerves. "There've been bruises, too. A couple of minor lumps on a couple of the women's heads, like he might have had to knock them around to subdue them. But cause of death has been blood loss and internal injuries from the knife attacks."

"He'd have had to subdue them so he could bind and gag them to get them out of their houses without neighbors noticing."

"Probably. Although he's been really careful about when he strikes. He usually works between ten and midnight, when most folks around here are already asleep. His victims are asleep and he attacks with no warning. And so far, he's managed to get to them when they're alone."

"Did any of the victims have security alarms?"

"Around here?" The look she gave him made him feel like an idiot. "Half the people around here never even lock their doors."

"That's crazy these days," he said with a shake of his head. "Even in a little bitty nowhere place like Bitterwood."

"Old habits. People want to believe they're safe, so they keep on behaving as if they are." She reached forward to wipe away the condensation starting to fog up the windshield.

"No." Sutton grabbed her wrist, stilling the motion. She turned to look at him, her dark eyes wide with surprise. Beneath his fingers her pulse beat like the wings of a trapped bird, swift and violent.

Desire licked at his belly like flames. He let go of her wrist, his heartbeat thundering in his ears. He swallowed and found his voice. "Better let 'em fog up. Makes it harder to see us inside, in case he's out there looking for a target."

She dropped her hand to her lap. It curled into a fist, her knuckles pressing hard against her thigh. She gazed forward at the opaque windshield, her chest rising and falling more swiftly than before.

The sudden whoop of a siren, close by, made them both give a start. The flash of blue and cherry lights painted the condensation on the passenger window with streaks of color. Sutton lowered the window to reveal a white-and-green Sevier County Sheriff's Department cruiser pulling up beside them. A man in his early thirties with sharp blue eyes and a close-shaved head gazed back at them, his expression wary.

"John," Ivy said, and the deputy's expression immediately cleared. He shot her a smile so friendly, so full of male appreciation, that Sutton felt the absurd urge to knock it right off his face.

John's smile died suddenly. "Good Lord, Hawkins, you're bleedin'! Did you get hit?"

No mention of the bloody shrapnel wound on Sutton's jaw, he noticed, not sure whether he was amused or pissed off by the omission.

"Just a scratch." Ivy pressed her fingertips to the nick. "John, I don't know if the shooter is still up there. He could be. I don't know how far he could have gotten in such a short time or whether he had a getaway vehicle parked over on the North Carolina side. You might want to see if you can get a chopper in the air and maybe give the Swain County boys over in North Carolina a heads-up."

"Chopper's on its way already, and the sheriff was on the phone with the Swain County sheriff last I talked to anyone at the station. Come on. Let's get the two of you somewhere safe and dry."

Sutton looked at Ivy. "See you in Sevierville?"

She reached out to catch his hand as he started to open the door. Her gaze was fathomless. "I'm not sure I'd have gotten off that mountain alive without you. Thanks."

As he let go of her hand and headed for his truck, he didn't remind her she wouldn't have been on the mountain in the first place if it weren't for him. Whether he said it aloud or not, Ivy Hawkins would figure it out on her own, sooner or later. She'd realize her mama had been right about him all along.

Calhouns were nothing but trouble.

"YOUR FELLOW ANY KIN to old Cleve Calhoun?" John Mallory touched the antiseptic-soaked cotton ball against the cut on Ivy's cheek, making her wince.

"Son," she answered with a wary glance up at him. She should have known the old man's reputation would have spread far past Bitterwood after so many years. "And he's not my fellow."

"Is he anything like his old man?"

She started to say no but stopped. What did she know about Sutton Calhoun these days, really? Hell, she hadn't even called Cooper Security to check his credentials, had she? Cleve Calhoun had made his reputation on the back of some of the biggest, most reasonable-sounding lies ever told. Maybe Sutton had followed in his daddy's footsteps, for all she knew. There was a lot she didn't know about his life after he left Bitterwood—and her—behind.

"That's to be determined," she answered John's question.

"Maybe someone figured he had a damn good reason to take a shot at him." Johnny's sharp eyes met hers with the hint of a smile in their crinkled corners. He put an adhesive bandage over the cut on her cheek. "My cousin Arlen lost a big chunk of change on one of old Cleve's land deals about a decade ago, and he hasn't ever really recovered, financially or otherwise. I reckon Arlen might want to take a shot or two at old Cleve, if he could still afford a rifle."

"So you think that was someone trying to send a message to my daddy through me?" Sutton's slow, amused drawl drew Ivy's gaze. He stood in the open doorway of the interrogation room where John had taken her to patch up her scratch. Someone had seen to his wound as well, applying a small, round bandage to the nick on his jaw.

"You tell me," John replied. "Who do *you* think shot at you?"

"I'm not sure." Sutton walked into the room at an unhurried pace. He studied John's first-aid handiwork through narrowed eyes before lifting his gaze to meet Ivy's. He smiled slightly, and once again, those smoldering hazel eyes made her gut twist into a hot, tight knot. "Any luck locating the shooter?"

"We found a few slugs stuck in trees up on the mountain, but looks like he policed his brass. We didn't find any spent shells. Or any sign of the shooter himself."

Sutton didn't look surprised. "So, are we free to go?"

Johnny put his hand on Ivy's shoulder. She dragged her gaze from Sutton's and looked at her old friend. "You sure you're okay to drive?" he asked.

She gave him a look that made him grin. "I'm fine to drive."

"I reckon y'all are free to go, then." He let go of her shoulder. "You might want to avoid meeting anonymous strangers at the top of Clingmans Dome in the future," he added as he walked them out to where they'd parked their vehicles. He bent and gave Ivy a quick kiss on her forehead. "That goes for you, too, Hawk." He walked them as far as the door leading to the parking lot and waved goodbye as they headed toward their vehicles.

"Boyfriend?" Sutton's tone was soft and bone-dry.

"Old church camp buddy," she answered, turning to look at him. The rain had stopped for the time being, though the heavy clouds overhead suggested the storm wasn't yet over. But her clothes were still damp through, and the cold wind blowing across the parking lot made her shiver.

Sutton pushed a strand of hair away from her face. "You

should get yourself home and get warm and dried out before you catch cold."

"I don't think you should stay at the motel again tonight," she said before she had finished forming the thought.

His eyebrows notched upward.

"The man with the rifle knows where you're staying," she explained. "What makes you think he's not lying in wait for you at the motel?"

He gave her a thoughtful look. "I guess nothing. It's a possibility."

"Do you have somewhere else you can stay? Maybe with Cleve?"

He shook his head. "Not going to happen."

She couldn't believe what she was about to suggest. Hadn't she just admitted to John that she didn't really know a damned thing about what Sutton Calhoun had become after he left Bitterwood? All she knew was the jumble of stories that passed around town like wildfire, and half of those were pure fantasy, in her experience.

But she said the words anyway. "So come stay at my house."

His eyes narrowed. "I thought your boss told you to stay clear of me."

"He said not to let you near my investigation," she admitted. "But you've already blown past that stop sign. And besides, I'm not letting him dictate what I do or who I see on my own time." The words came out sounding more like a challenge than she'd intended.

The look he gave her set fire to her toes. The rush of heat spread upward until she felt as if her whole body were on fire.

"Okay," he said.

Oh, hell.

Chapter Five

"I don't rightly remember what he looked like." The Stay and Save night clerk, a skinny young man in his early twenties who looked as if he might be a little stoned, answered Sutton's question with a wrinkled brow, as if trying to remember what had happened less than twenty-four hours earlier was too much of a mental strain.

Hell, it probably was.

"And you're sure it was a man who left the message?" Sutton glanced at Ivy, whose expression shifted at his question. Apparently she'd been making the same assumption he had, that the gunman in the woods was a man. But assumptions could be wrong.

Just not this time, apparently. "Definitely a man," the clerk said with a firm nod. "I remember the voice was deep. Definitely a guy. But, see, I was filling out some paperwork that's due at the end of this week, and it's really complicated, so I didn't take time to look up to see his face. I just jotted down what he told me to and then got back to my paperwork."

Damned inconvenient, Sutton thought. "Could you tell anything from his voice? His ethnicity or where he might be from?"

The clerk squinted, as if trying to remember was hard. "I don't remember any accent, so I guess that probably means he's from somewhere around these parts. I think he was white. I guess he could have been Cherokee, since we get some of those around here sometimes, too. Pretty sure he wasn't black." He looked up at Sutton, his forehead smoothing out. "Yeah, he wasn't black. I kinda saw him out of the corner of my eye, and I think I'd have noticed whether he was black or white."

"Do you remember if he was tall? Short? Heavy or thin?"

"Kinda tall," the clerk answered after a moment of thought. "He blocked out some of the light in the doorway, so he must have been tall. I'd say average build. Not fat, not skinny. Really, though, that's all I remember." He looked up at Sutton with a hint of pleading, as if asking them not to make him put his brain to use any more tonight.

Ivy took mercy on him. "If you remember anything else about the person who left the note for Mr. Calhoun, please give me a call at the police station." She stepped forward and handed the clerk her card. "Thanks for your help."

With a gesture of her head toward Sutton, she headed out of the office.

He followed her out to where they'd parked the Jeep and the Ranger. He'd already grabbed his things from the room while she'd stood guard outside, looking like a tiny soldier with her gun hanging from the holster at her side. His bags were stowed away on the bench seat of his truck.

He was already beginning to regret saying yes to Ivy's rash offer of a place to stay. If he found himself lusting after her in the middle of a bullet-flying ambush, what chance did he have to be on his best behavior holed up with her in a cozy little house for a few days? And he was probably putting her job in jeopardy as well just by being there.

But the Stay and Save was the only motel in Bitterwood. There was a bed-and-breakfast on the other side of town, but he'd checked. It was booked through the next week. The next-closest place to stay was almost all the way to Maryville—not that long a drive, really, but conducting his investigation from a town over would be a pain in the neck.

Maybe he should suck up his courage and see if Cleve would put him up for a few days. He'd lived with his father for eighteen years. What were a few more days?

"I'm kind of glad you're going to be staying with me," Ivy said as he opened the driver's door of the truck. In the harsh lighting of the motel parking lot, her small face was cast in chiaroscuro, her eyes hidden by inky shadows, making it impossible for him to read her expression.

"Why's that?" he asked.

"Easier to keep an eye on you," she said with a half smile. Her tone of voice reminded him of his lingering impression of the girl who'd been his friend all those years ago—feisty, surprising and brutally honest.

He followed the taillights of her Jeep to a small house on Vesper Road, a winding road that led through the woods at the base of Smoky Ridge. In the beams of their headlights, he got an impression of a neat, well-kept house with pale gray exterior paint and bright yellow trim.

Smiling at the quirky juxtaposition of subdued and vibrant, he wondered if she'd been the one to choose the paint colors. It seemed to suit her own contradictions, the interplay of control and impulse that had driven her to follow him all the way to Clingmans Dome that evening.

Maybe she hadn't changed all that much over the years. The odd, thoughtful girl who'd become his sounding board and loyal champion when they were little more than kids had been a mass of contradictions as well, both fiercely brave and painfully shy, whip-smart and endearingly naive.

God, he'd missed her like crazy those first few lonely

days away from Bitterwood and everything he'd ever known.

Behind her house, the looming, dark contours of Smoky Ridge towered over the valley below like a silent, ancient sentry. As children, he and Ivy had both lived on that mountain. She, like he, had played among the firs and spruce, explored the natural caves and climbed the soaring ridges until they could see for miles and miles around them.

When he'd left here years ago, he'd been certain nothing in these hills had the power to draw him back. Not even Ivy. Even a few days ago, when Jesse Cooper had assigned him to work with Stephen Billings on the investigation into his sister's murder, Sutton hadn't believed there was anything about Bitterwood that could speak to him anymore.

But he'd been wrong. The land itself was a potent reminder that there had been beauty among the ruins of his childhood. Happiness that even misery hadn't destroyed.

And there had been Ivy Hawkins, who'd understood him without having to be told what he was feeling. He hadn't realized how much he had missed having someone in his life he could trust that way.

Ivy parked the Jeep in the driveway, leaving room for him to pull up parallel with her. She waited on the driveway for him to get out of the truck, greeting him with an oddly anxious smile.

"This is it." She looked at the house and back at him.

"I like it," he said truthfully.

Her pleased look made his chest ache a little. "It's not very big, but I have a spare room with a fold-out bed you can use. Are you hungry? I'm starving." She started down the walkway to the house at a brisk clip, forcing him to move quickly to catch up at the door.

Inside, the house was surprisingly cozy for a place be-

longing to an unmarried cop who lived alone. The front
door opened into a small den decorated in warm shades
of brown, green and amber. Despite the almost utilitarian
lines of the furnishings, feminine touches surprised the
eye here and there—a pair of lacy throw pillows in a deep
shade of crimson tossed on each end of the brown leather
sofa, a dreamy impressionist landscape hanging over the
river-stone hearth, a pair of fuzzy yellow slippers lying
at the foot of the overstuffed armchair near the window.

He felt Ivy's gaze on his face, as if she was waiting for
his reaction. He looked at her and smiled just to see her
smile back at him. "I like it inside, too. It feels like a home."

Her cheeks went pink as she bent to pick up a magazine
that lay open on the coffee table. He caught a glimpse of
a colorful garden on the front of the magazine before she
deposited it into a wood rack by the sofa, where it joined
a small pile of other magazines. "I'm not sure I spend
enough time here for it to really feel like a home," she admitted, unbuckling her shoulder holster as she crossed to
a tall, four-drawer chest standing near an open archway
that seemed to lead into a hall. She withdrew the Smith &
Wesson from the holster, unlocked a drawer that contained
a gun case and locked the pistol inside.

"You don't keep a gun nearby at all times?" Sutton's
own pistol felt like an appendage to him. He'd learned
never to get caught without it. Fortunately, Tennessee hon-
ored his Alabama concealed carry license. He wouldn't
have wanted to come back to Bitterwood unarmed.

The Calhouns had made too many enemies over the
past few generations for him to walk around unprotected.

"That's my work-issued sidearm," she answered with
a little grin that made his gut clench with pure male hunger. She unlocked the second drawer down and pulled out
another case. Inside lay a compact Glock 26. She checked

the chamber and the magazine, then held it up to show Sutton. "This is my personal weapon."

She put the Glock in an unattached ankle holster. "You hungry?"

"Yeah, but mostly I'm cold and wet," he admitted. "I could use a shower and change of clothes before food."

Her gaze lifted slowly to meet his, mysteries roiling in those dark brown eyes. "There's a bathroom down the hall." She pointed him in the right direction. "The spare room is right next to that. It's a little cluttered but the fold-out sofa is pretty comfortable. I'll get you some sheets when you're ready to bunk down."

By the time he had showered and changed into warmer clothes, Ivy had somehow managed to do the same, for when he found her in the kitchen, looking through her pantry, her hair was twisted into a towel turban. The jeans were gone, replaced by a pair of black yoga pants under a long-sleeved UT-Chattanooga T-shirt. She smelled like green apples.

"I'm thinking a cup of nice hot soup and maybe a grilled cheese sandwich?" She looked over her shoulder at him for his input.

"Sounds great," he agreed. "I could make the sandwiches while you heat up the soup. Just point me to a pan."

They worked in efficient silence for the next few moments, and as the rumbling of his stomach began to overcome the hot-and-bothered feeling he'd gotten at the sight and smell of a freshly showered Ivy Hawkins, Sutton began to think he might be able to handle all this forced togetherness after all.

For one night, at least.

"I don't think they'll find the shooter," Ivy said a few minutes later as she poured steaming tomato soup into a couple of mugs. "Do you?"

"Probably not," he agreed. He handed her a plate holding a crispy grilled cheese sandwich. He still hadn't quite wrapped his mind around who the shooter could be. He'd been in plenty of dangerous hot spots over the past decade or so, made a few enemies, at least in the abstract. But Special Forces operatives toiled mostly in anonymity.

"Do you know anyone who might want you dead?" Ivy sat at the small breakfast nook table and waved at the opposite chair, inviting him to take a seat. She wrapped her hands around the mug of soup, making a contented noise deep in her throat, undermining Sutton's earlier confidence that his sleepover at Ivy's would be easier than expected.

"I was just thinking about that," he admitted. "I'm sure I did things while I was in the army that might earn me some enemies. But none of them ever knew my real name. I was never captured, never had my story written up in a newspaper. I was the mystery man in the civvies and beard—they probably thought I was CIA rather than Special Forces."

Ivy's eyes narrowed slightly at his answer, and he wondered what she was thinking. He'd always been pretty good at reading people's thoughts in their expressions and their body language, but Ivy Hawkins kept her emotions and thoughts well hidden these days. He wondered how much of that particular talent had come as a natural result of covering up for a sexually promiscuous mother with dangerous taste in men. How many lies had she been forced to tell just to keep the Department of Children's Services away from her door?

He'd told a few lies like that in his day, especially after his mother died. His growing disdain for his father's con games had been eclipsed only by the fear of getting sucked into the foster care system. He'd known kids in Bitterwood who'd been pulled onto that particular governmental merry-go-round, and he'd promised himself he'd put up with anything Cleve might do as long as he didn't have to leave home and go live with strangers.

Of course, the first thing he'd done the second he'd left Bitterwood behind was sign up for the army and spend the next months and years putting his life in the hands of strangers who wore the same uniform he did.

"You don't think it could have anything to do with the murders, do you?" Ivy asked.

"I don't see how. Not many people even know I'm back in town, much less that I'm investigating April Billings's murder."

"Word flies pretty fast in a small town." She took a sip of the soup and gave another soft murmur of pleasure that made Sutton's jeans feel two sizes too tight. Worse, he'd just realized she wasn't wearing a bra under that snug-fitting T-shirt.

Why the hell couldn't he get sex off his mind around her?

A faint trilling noise came from somewhere nearby. Ivy sighed and crossed to the table where she'd left her purse. Digging her cell phone from one of the inner pockets, she answered. "Hawkins."

Another murder? Sutton edged forward in his chair, keeping his eye on Ivy's face, trying to read her expression.

Her face remained carefully neutral. "Yes, thank you for calling me back tonight. Can you hold for a moment?" She put her hand over the phone speaker and looked at Sutton. "Excuse me. I have to take this call." She walked into one of the rooms off the living room and closed the door.

He released a slow breath and looked down at his uneaten food, his gut in knots. He'd never let a woman derail him from anything he put his mind to, and he'd been involved with his share of smart, sexy women, in the service and out. So why was Ivy turning him inside out all of a sudden?

She was pretty. Curvy and physically fit. Gutsy to a fault. And she had a bright, inquisitive mind he'd always found appealing, even when they'd been kids. But none of those attributes should have been enough to make a man his age with his experience feel so off-kilter.

He made himself eat his sandwich, washing it down with the cooling soup. Maybe hunger and a lack of sleep were behind his out-of-sorts feeling. It was already after ten, and he hadn't had any sleep in over twenty-four hours. Since Ivy showed no sign of coming out of her bedroom anytime soon, he decided to find the linen closet himself and make up the fold-out bed without bothering her.

And then he'd do his damnedest to get a good night's sleep, despite the proximity of Ivy Hawkins's cotton-clad curves. Hell, he'd slept through firefights before.

He could sleep through an untimely case of lust.

"I'M SORRY TO DISTURB you so late." Ivy kept her voice low so that it wouldn't carry outside her bedroom.

"I was working late," the man on the other end of the line assured her. He had a deep voice, with a bit of a Southern drawl. He'd identified himself as Jesse Cooper, CEO of Cooper Security. Ivy had left a message for Cooper while she was waiting for Sutton to finish his statement to the Sevier County Sheriff's Department. "You wanted information about Sutton Calhoun?"

Now that she'd finally reached the head of Cooper Security, she felt odd asking questions about Sutton. "Mr. Calhoun is peripherally involved in a murder investigation, and I wanted to confirm his account of his reason for being here in Bitterwood."

"What has he told you?" Jesse Cooper sounded cautious.

"Why do I get the feeling you'd back up anything I told you Sutton had said?" Ivy sat on the edge of her bed and closed her eyes, her head aching. She needed food and sleep, in that order, and Jesse Cooper's obvious reluctance to be open with her wasn't helping.

"We have to maintain a certain amount of discretion for our clients." Cooper sounded genuinely apologetic. "That means I have to trust my agents to share only what they feel they must about the cases they're on."

"Has he told you that he was the target of an ambush tonight?" Almost as soon as the words came out of her mouth, she felt like a tattletale. But she needed to know if Sutton had a price on his head. Not just for his sake but also for the sake of the townspeople she'd sworn to protect.

"Was he injured?"

"No, he's fine," she quickly assured him.

"Did you apprehend the suspect?"

"No," she answered more reluctantly. "He was shooting from a distance and by the time the Sevier County Sheriff's Department arrived to do a fugitive search, he'd apparently left the area."

"And you're concerned Sutton poses a danger to your town?"

"Does he?"

"Not that I know of."

She didn't find his tone reassuring. "Cooper Security has a reputation as a trouble magnet."

"When you try to stop powerful, dangerous people, that's what happens, Detective Hawkins."

Now she felt guilty about doubting Sutton. But she had to know if she could trust him.

"I realize the Calhoun name doesn't exactly foster trust in your neck of the woods," Cooper added. "And I get it. I know the family history. But Sutton Calhoun isn't his father. I have no complaints about his work. And I wouldn't have hired him if I didn't believe he could be trusted. Does that set your mind at ease?"

"Yes," she admitted. "I just had to know."

"Now you do." Cooper's tone was kind. "And if there's anything we can do to help you, let me know."

She gave a soft huff of laughter. "I don't think the Bitterwood Police Department can afford your rates, Mr. Cooper. But I appreciate the thought."

She hung up and slumped on the edge of the bed, staring at her closed door. What had she been expecting, to hear that Sutton was lying?

Or was that what she'd been hoping? Had she been looking for a reason to kick him out of her house before she ended up falling head over heels for him the way she had when she was just fifteen and he didn't see her as anything but a friend?

Too bad. He was on the up-and-up. She'd just have to control her emotions the hard way.

With a weary grumble, she pushed to her feet and opened the door, prepared to apologize to Sutton for taking so long. But when she entered the kitchen, she found he was no longer sitting at the breakfast nook.

"Sutton?"

"In here." His voice came from the spare room down the hall.

She followed his voice and found him sitting up in the fold-out bed, covered up to his bare torso. His smoldering gaze lifted to meet hers.

Her knees trembled and she sneaked a hand out to grab the door frame. "I'm sorry. That took longer than I expected. I see you found the sheets."

"Yeah."

"I, uh—" Whatever she'd been planning to say drifted

away like smoke on the wind as her reckless gaze drifted away from his hazel eyes to settle on his chest. He was lean and toned, with well-defined muscles that didn't look as if they'd been built through reps on a weight machine at the local gym. Dark hair sprinkled his chest and converged in a dusky line that disappeared beneath the sheet.

She made herself look away. "Do you have everything you need?"

He took so long to answer she couldn't help meeting his gaze again. "I think so," he answered in a tone of voice that suggested there was at least one thing he didn't have and wanted very much.

"Okay," she said, barely able to hear her own voice over the sudden thunderous pounding of her pulse in her ears. "Well, good night."

"Good night," he murmured, his scorching gaze branding her.

She forced her feet backward, out of the room, and pulled the door shut behind her. She stood with her hand on the doorknob, taking a couple of deep breaths.

Too little sleep, too much stress, she told herself as her fingers tightened on the cool metal of the doorknob. That was her problem. A good night's sleep would give her back a sense of perspective.

But when she slept, she dreamed.

SHE LAY TANGLED IN yellow sheets that looked blue in the moonlight pouring through the bedroom window. Her blanket lay in a puddle on the floor, kicked away as she dreamed.

She dressed like a child, he thought, her woman's body clad in soft cotton pants and a T-shirt that could have passed for pajamas. He didn't know if he found the appearance of innocence disappointing or exciting.

Exciting, he decided. Although maybe it was the prospect of bathing himself in her blood that sent his pulse racing with anticipation.

The window was unlocked, as he'd known it would be. He was a man of remarkable luck as well as thoughtful planning. Things had a way of working out for him in just the way he needed, though he was surprised, in a way, because of who she was.

The detective. The steely-eyed law-woman who should have known the importance of checking all the doors and windows before she went to bed. Perhaps she'd lived too long in this bucolic little mountain hamlet and had, like others before her, bought into the foolish notion that nothing bad could happen in a place so beautiful.

On the table by her bedside, a file folder lay open. He moved closer, his eyes so well-adjusted to the dark that he could see the folder's contents with little effort. Photographs of bodies. His handiwork.

Excitement flaring in the pit of his gut, he flipped through the file. Hastily compiled dossiers on each victim followed the photographs. April Billings. Amelia Sanderson. Coral Vines. The new one, Marjorie Kenner.

She was trying to connect them, but the pieces just weren't there. But she was close. So close.

Picking up the pen lying by the dossier, he bent and jotted a note on the inside of the folder. He stared at the single word, smiling. Would anyone know what it meant?

He walked silently to the side of her bed and gazed down at her. A disappointment, in a way. He'd hoped for more of a challenge.

Looming closer, he stretched his hand toward her. His shadow drifted across her face, plunging her sleep-softened features into darkness. A shame. He had wanted to see her face when she realized her time had run out.

Her soft respiration was the only sound in the room. He let it fill his ears, knowing it would soon die away forever.

With a violent thrust, he closed his hand over her throat and squeezed.

Ivy woke in a rush, phantom fingers pressing against the flesh of her neck. She reached for them before she realized she had only been dreaming.

A low moan of relief escaping her throat, she sat up and pressed her face into her hands, willing her racing heart back to a normal rhythm. Already, the nightmare was beginning to dissipate, but she tried to hold on to the images. Something—there was something…

When her legs stopped shaking, she pushed herself off the bed and padded barefoot across the cold hardwood floor to her window, fumbling for the brass window latch.

It was safely locked in place.

She slumped with relief, pressing her forehead against the cold glass pane. Outside, the night had gone quiet, the worst of the storm now past. A pale hint of moon glow peeked through the thinning clouds, casting a blue square of light across the wood slats of her front porch.

Suddenly, a shadow moved across the patch of light, quick and furtive.

A shadow shaped like a man.

Chapter Six

As tired as he was, Sutton had hoped he'd fall asleep quickly. Anything to keep from lying there, just a few feet from where Ivy Hawkins was sleeping, imagining in vivid detail what it would be like to explore every inch of her curvy little body.

He was used to sleeping wherever he laid his head, in desert or jungle, soft hotel bed or grimy blanket on the cold and stony ground. But he couldn't relax enough to close his eyes for long, and it took a while to realize that his insomnia was about more than his libido. He was also worrying over the meaning of the evening's ambush.

Why *had* someone targeted him? As he'd pointed out to Ivy, not many people even knew he was in town, and even if a few folks had seen him around and recognized the Calhoun boy who'd left town nearly fifteen years ago, how many would know he was investigating one of the murders?

Or was Ivy's friend John the deputy right? Could the shooter have targeted him for being Cleve Calhoun's son?

But why not target Cleve instead? As far as Sutton knew, his father didn't exactly live holed up behind a fortress wall. If someone wanted him dead badly enough, it shouldn't have been hard to make it happen.

The darkness outside the spare room window had softened, a hint of moonlight drifting through the curtains as it struggled to penetrate the wispy remainder of storm clouds darkening the sky. From where he lay on the sofa bed, Sutton could make out the outline of spiky evergreen treetops, black against the fainter blue of the sky.

Suddenly, a flash of darkness blotted out the pale light. Just as suddenly, it was gone and the light was back.

Sutton sat up in a single, fluid motion, one hand reaching for the Glock 17 lying on the nicked wooden table by the sofa. He padded quietly to the window that looked out on the front yard. The porch was empty, as was the patch of grass beyond. Scudding clouds swallowed the moon again, pitching the night into inky darkness. But Sutton felt, more than saw, movement outside. A furtive, slinking shadow glided just beyond the edges of his vision until it faded into the blackness of the tree line at the edge of the yard.

He heard the front door open with a soft creak. Taking just enough time to pull on his jeans and shove his feet into a pair of running shoes, he hurried out to the front room in time to see the door close with a soft snick.

Had someone come in? Or gone out?

Carefully, he eased open the door. The groan of the hinges made him wince. So much for stealth.

"Stop there." Ivy's voice was a low growl in the impenetrable darkness.

"It's me," he whispered quickly.

"I saw someone pass by the window." She kept her voice low, but the whisper couldn't hide the tension in her tone.

"I did, too." He realized he was still holding the Glock outstretched. He dropped it to his side.

"I might have seen someone moving out by the trees, but I can't be sure." Ivy moved, a dark shape looming toward him in the dark. He felt the heat of her body as it neared his, a potent reminder that the night had grown

cold and damp, making him wish he'd taken a moment
more to grab a shirt.

Suddenly, her small, dark shape pitched forward with a
gasp, slamming into him. He put up his free hand to catch
her, and the soft heat of her body burned into his bare skin
like a brand.

"So sorry!' she breathed against his chest, steadying
herself by grasping both his arms. "I stepped on something that made me trip—"

Damn, she felt good. Soft in all the right places, and
sweet-smelling, like ripe apples warmed by the sun. A few
strands of her hair still clung to his face, caught in his beard
stubble, the sensation unexpectedly arousing.

He let go of her reluctantly when she stepped away and
bent to pick up something at her feet.

"Hmm," she said, her tone puzzled. He heard a soft click
and the beam of a flashlight sliced through the gloom, almost blinding him for a second.

It took a moment for his eyesight to adjust enough to see
what she held between her thumb and forefinger. It was a
small marble, the stone orb a unique swirl of bright lime-
green and darker teal. Sutton's breath caught for a hitch as
he realized he'd seen the marble before.

A long, long time ago.

"This is what I tripped on." Ivy turned the marble over
and over, studying the twists of color as if she could find
an answer there. "Looks like a kid's marble."

"It is," Sutton said, his mind reeling through the impli-
cations of this particular marble showing up here on this
particular night. His gaze slid back out to the dark tree line
where he thought he'd seen movement earlier. The darkness was still and silent now. If someone had been out there
before, he was long gone now.

But there was no *if* about it, was there? Someone *had* been here. Someone had left that marble.

And he knew who.

He realized Ivy was looking at him. He met her curious gaze in the ambient glow of the flashlight. "It's mine," he added. That much wasn't a lie. The marble had belonged to him once, many years ago.

Ivy's brow creased a little more deeply. "You carry a marble around? What, like a good luck charm or something?"

He took the marble from her fingers and dropped it in his pocket. "Guess it didn't turn out so lucky for you. Sorry it tripped you."

Her puzzled expression didn't clear right away. "No harm done."

"You know, if we saw anyone," he added, already moving toward the door, "it was probably some kids or something. Maybe they'd planned to play a prank until you scared them off."

"Yeah, maybe." Ivy followed him slowly back inside, still looking thoughtful. "You go on back to bed. I'm going to check all the doors and windows before I hit the sack again."

He should offer to go with her, to make sure the place was locked down securely, but the green marble seemed to be burning a hole in his pocket. He gave in to his roiling curiosity and went back to the spare room, closing the door behind him so he could figure out in peace what to do next.

He checked his watch. Almost midnight. Which would make it eleven back in Chickasaw County. Late, but not egregiously so. He picked up his cell phone and dialed Delilah Hammond's cell number.

She answered in a sleepy growl after two rings. "Damn

it, Sutton, just because you can't sleep doesn't mean the rest of us can't."

"I know you said you never hear from Seth, but do you ever hear anything about him? Maybe what he's doing these days or where he is?"

She was silent a moment. "What makes you ask that now?"

He considered telling her about the marble, then remembered she hadn't known anything about Seth's con job back then. Sutton had been suckered out of that marble thanks to his own stupidity as much as Seth's duplicity, and he hadn't wanted to admit his mistake to anyone.

"I guess it's just being back here in Bitterwood," he answered instead. "Makes me nostalgic for the old days."

"Seth hasn't been your friend in a lot of years." She sounded more puzzled than defensive.

"I know. I just wondered if you had any idea where he was these days or what he was doing."

She paused again before answering. "He's in Maryville now. At least, that's what he told me when he called this afternoon."

Sutton sank onto the edge of the bed, his gut tightening with dismay. Maryville was a short, easy drive from Bitterwood. Not far from Clingmans Dome, either. "He called you this afternoon? Out of the blue?"

"Yeah. Said he'd been thinking about me and wanted me to know where to find him if I ever needed him. Says he's got a real job. Legit." Her hopeful tone made Sutton's stomach ache. Even though Delilah was a smart, sensible woman who knew her brother as well as anyone, there was a part of her that wanted to believe he'd changed, as unlikely a possibility as it might be. Sometimes love was more free with second chances than was wise.

"Where's he working now?"

"Some trucking company there in Maryville." She stifled a yawn. "I wrote it down—wait a sec—here. Davenport Trucking in Maryville. You thinking of looking him up?"

Sutton looked at the green marble nestled in the curve of his palm. The teal threads of color inside the green marble seemed to glow with light. "Yeah," he answered, closing his fist over the marble. "I think I will."

ALL OF THE WINDOWS and doors were safely locked. Ivy wasn't sure why she'd made such a big deal of double-checking them. She'd just had a strong feeling she should. To be sure.

As she slid between the sheets again and reached for the switch to turn off the light, her gaze fell on the folder lying on her bedside table. It was closed, which surprised her for some reason.

She dropped her hand from the light switch and picked up the folder. Balancing it on her knees, she opened it and looked at the photos and notes inside. April Billings's photo was on the top of the stack. Not the crime scene photo but a recent posed photo of the pretty young college student provided by the family. "I want you to remember her as a person, not just a body," April's mother had told Ivy when she handed over her daughter's photo. It had been the day she'd talked the captain into letting her join forces with Antoine Parsons on the murders.

There had been three homicides by that time—the two earlier cases Antoine had been investigating and the newer one Ivy had taken the lead on. She was convinced the three cases were related, and Antoine had agreed. Only the captain thought differently, and he'd been reluctant to combine the investigations.

She'd expressed curiosity to Antoine about the captain's

recalcitrance, but Antoine had told her it was all about turf. The captain didn't want the TBI or the feds nosing around the Bitterwood Police Department, asking inconvenient questions about how they did things in the sticks.

"You think there's corruption going on?" Ivy had asked.

"I don't know, and I've learned not to ask any questions," Antoine had answered flatly. "I just do my job and make sure the cases I work don't get corrupted by office politics. I suggest you do the same."

She moved on past April Billings's files and found the next victim. Amelia Sanderson. Age thirty. Mousy brown hair worn in a messy short bob. In the crime scene photos, she was lying faceup in bed, half-open eyes staring, sightless, at some infinite point beyond the camera's range. A pair of wire-rim glasses lay on the bedside table. No blood on them, no fingerprints but Amelia's found when the crime scene unit dusted them. Like April Billings, she'd been killed elsewhere and returned, nearly bloodless, to her bed.

Ivy flipped past the photo and read over the short bio Antoine had compiled. She was a bookkeeper, working for a trucking company in Maryville. Davenport Trucking.

She paused, an image flitting through her mind. A word scrawled on the inside cover of the manila folder.

Davenport.

She flipped back to the front cover and looked for the handwritten note, but the folder was bare. Checking the back as well, she found it also empty.

But the image was so vivid in her mind now. Those nine letters, written in sprawling ink across the folder.

By the killer.

Her hand trembling, she closed her eyes, searching the image that seemed imprinted on her mind. Saw the hand moving down to the open folder, watched the pen strokes form on the manila and realized, with a little shiver, that while the hand was large and male, the handwriting was her own.

Her subconscious sending her a message?

She moved forward to the third victim, Coral Vines. Coral's murder had been Ivy's case, and if she hadn't been following Antoine's investigation of the other two murders out of sheer curiosity, she might not have made the connection between those deaths and that of Coral Vines. Of the four women killed, Coral lived in a seedier part of town, her lifestyle one that might lend itself to random homicide more easily than being a college student on summer break or a retired high school librarian with no enemies outside of a few disgruntled former students with big late fines.

Coral Vines, twenty-eight and widowed, drank too much, according to friends and family alike. The death of her husband in Afghanistan a few years earlier had sent her over a ledge, it seemed, and she eased her pain with whiskey and classic Southern rock played at ear-bursting decibels on a bad drinking night. Whatever job she'd once had she'd lost and was living on welfare and the kindness of friends.

But she'd worked at some point, Ivy thought, flipping back through the bio. She vaguely remembered someone mentioning a job and how she'd lost it because of the drinking.

There. She found it jotted on the margin of the typed-up bio. "Worked as a billing secretary—Davenport, Maryville."

Davenport Trucking again?

She flipped back to the bio Antoine had compiled on April Billings. Most of the notes were about her college career. No mention of whether she'd picked up a job this summer while she was home from college.

But April's brother had hired Sutton Calhoun to look into her murder. Would Sutton know?

She grabbed her threadbare robe and wrapped it around herself before she ventured down the hall to the spare room. She paused for a moment, listening for any sounds from within.

Suddenly, the door whipped open and Sutton almost walked right into her. She stumbled backward in surprise, bumping her head hard against the wall across the hall. "Ow."

His look of surprise settled into mild concern. "You okay?"

She rubbed the aching spot on the back of her head. "Yeah, you just surprised me. Do you need something?"

"Just a glass of water." His expression was a neutral mask, impossible to read. She didn't know if he was telling the truth or hiding something—by design, she suspected. Her gaze wandered down to his bare chest, and all thoughts of truth or secrets flew out of her head for a long, heart-fluttering moment.

Since when was she so vulnerable to lean-muscled pecs and a flat, well-defined belly?

Since Sutton Calhoun brought his bad-boy self into your house, reminding you of how it feels to be fifteen and madly in love with the juiciest piece of forbidden fruit to ever grow in Bitterwood, Tennessee.

"What were you doing outside my door?" he asked when she didn't say anything else.

She jerked her attention back to the case. "I was looking through the case files on the murders, actually," she said, nodding her head toward the kitchen. She walked with him down the short corridor into the kitchen, pointing him to the water glasses over the stove. "I came across something I'd missed before."

"Yeah?"

"Two of the victims worked at the same place, as it

turns out." She started to tell him about Davenport Trucking, then remembered Captain Rayburn's warning not to try to bring Sutton into the investigation. She was going to be in enough trouble as it was, once the captain heard about her Clingmans Dome adventure. Better keep the details to herself for now. "Anyway, I was wondering if maybe April Billings's brother had mentioned whether she'd taken a temporary job this summer while she was home from college."

Sutton turned away from the refrigerator, withdrawing his glass from the water dispenser in the door. He took a long drink of water, then shook his head. "Stephen didn't mention a job. I can ask."

"Thanks, I'd appreciate it. It may be nothing—this is a small rural area with limited job opportunities. Still, it's curious."

"Yeah." He drained his glass of water and put it in the sink. "I've got another lead to follow tomorrow, but I'll give Mr. Billings a call and let you know."

She walked with him to the spare room. "Another lead?"

"May be nothing. I want to follow it through before I say one way or another." He paused in the open doorway. "Get some sleep, Detective. You look beat." He closed the door behind him.

She stared at the solid rectangle of wood, releasing a sigh. Great. While she'd spent the past few minutes trying not to salivate over his bare chest, he thought she looked beat.

Nothing quite like abject humiliation at—she checked her watch—twelve twenty-five in the morning.

Sutton hadn't expected to sleep that night, but he must have drifted off at some point, because the next time he opened his eyes, his room was bright with morning sunlight. He glanced at his watch lying on the bedside table. Already after eight. He'd overslept.

Tugging his dirty jeans on, he checked the house and found a note from Ivy written on the back of a business card she'd pinned to the refrigerator with a black bear magnet. "Gone to work. Help yourself to eggs or anything else you want for breakfast."

Finding the coffeemaker on the counter next to the stove, he made himself a couple of cups of strong black coffee and cracked a couple of eggs into a skillet for an omelet. A shower and shave later, he dressed in jeans and a T-shirt and set out in the Ford Ranger for Maryville, the small city about twenty minutes southwest of Bitterwood. He'd looked up the address for Davenport Trucking on his phone and arrived on West Sperry Road to find the trucking company was a sprawling warehouse-style office complex in the middle of an otherwise rural area just outside the city. From the parking lot, the rounded peaks of Chilhowee Mountain formed a velvety blue horizon to the east.

Sutton stood by his truck for a moment, gazing at the mountains, struck by a powerful ache that settled in the middle of his chest. He hadn't called Bitterwood home in years, but the Smokies still had the power to steal his breath with their sheer blue beauty.

He dragged his gaze away and crossed the parking lot to the glass door marked Main Office. As he entered, a bell on the door clattered overhead. A slim black woman in her thirties looked up and smiled. "Can I help you?"

Before he could answer, the bell rang over the door behind him. He turned at the sound, his eyes widening at the sight of the newcomer.

Ivy Hawkins stood in the doorway, staring at him. Her expression shifted from surprise to suspicion, her dark eyes snapping. "What the hell are you doing here?"

Chapter Seven

It took a second for Sutton to school his features into his customary inscrutable mask, but it was enough. Ivy saw a ripple of guilt pass over his face before he shuttered his expression. At the same time, he seemed genuinely surprised to see her here.

"I came to look up an old friend," he answered, his voice carefully void of inflection.

"Yeah? What old friend?"

She noted the slight tightening of his mouth before he answered. "Seth Hammond. His sister said he's working here now."

Since when was Seth Hammond a friend? Sure, Sutton and Seth had been tight as ticks when they were boys, but by the time Sutton shook the dust of Bitterwood off his boots, he and Seth had been enemies.

"Why are *you* here?" Sutton asked.

"Following up a lead."

"This is the company you were talking about." Sutton's brow furrowed.

"Coincidence, huh?"

He looked a little defensive. "Yeah, definitely a coincidence."

"You're looking for Seth Hammond?" the receptionist

behind the desk interrupted. "He's probably out in the fleet garage. Third building on the right."

"Thanks." Sutton turned back to Ivy. "I'll head on out there now."

"Wait." Ivy caught his arm as he started to pass her.

He gazed down at her with hazel-eyed intensity that made her insides tremble. "Yeah?"

"Seth Hammond works here?"

"Looks like."

"When did you find that out? I thought you didn't know where he was anymore."

"I talked to his sister last night and she mentioned he was living here in Maryville now, working for Davenport Trucking. I thought I should drop by and say hello, see if he's really on the straight and narrow this time. For Delilah's sake." He cocked his head slightly. "What's your lead?"

She was tempted to tell him, if for no other reason than to make sure she wasn't simply grasping at straws about the Davenport connection. But she couldn't just go around spilling all her operational secrets to virtual strangers, no matter how good her memories were—or how damned hot he looked in a pair of jeans. "I'm not at liberty to discuss it."

He nodded slowly. "Okay."

She softened her tone. "Did you find anything to eat this morning?"

He smiled. "I might have raided your egg bin for an omelet."

She smiled back. "Feel free to raid the rest of the fridge for lunch if you like."

"Actually, I was thinking about grabbing something at J.T.'s Barbecue on my way back to Bitterwood," he said. "Think you'll be finished here by lunchtime?"

"Probably."

"Why don't I hang around then?" he suggested. "We can grab lunch together."

"Okay," she agreed, trying not to grin like an idiot. She watched him leave, her gaze dropping helplessly to his denim-clad backside.

Behind her, the receptionist let out a deep sigh. "That man sure can wear the hell out of a pair of jeans."

Ivy turned to look at the receptionist, biting back a grin. She crossed to the desk and flashed her shield. "I'm Ivy Hawkins with the Bitterwood Police Department. I have some questions about a couple of former employees. Who do I talk to?"

THE MAINTENANCE GARAGE two doors down from the main office turned out to be an enormous one-story building with tall retractable doors built in to accommodate a variety of trucks, from local delivery box vans to large eighteen-wheel big rigs.

When Sutton entered the garage, only four trucks were parked inside, two big rigs with full trailers, a large box truck with a local moving company's logo painted on the sides and a black panel van. A lone man occupied the space, holding a heavy-duty hose with a nozzle attachment at the end. Spray shot from the hose and hit the panel van's wheels with a loud splatter, the whoosh drowning out all but the faintest sound of the tune he was whistling. Water ran in a stream past Sutton's feet, rusty with red clay from the van's tires. He avoided the flow and crossed the garage to the man holding the hose.

He was wiry, hard-muscled but whipcord lean, with short, dark hair that tended to spike on top and sharply defined features that gave him a faintly vulpine appearance. His green eyes swept up to meet Sutton's gaze, and a slow, cynical smile curved his wide mouth.

He turned off the hose. The garage fell silent for a moment. Then the man spoke in a deceptively soft drawl. "Sutton Calhoun. Never thought I'd see you 'round these parts again."

"Really, Seth? That's how you want to play this?"

Seth Hammond's left eyebrow twitched. "What are you talking about?"

So innocent. If Sutton didn't know better, he might believe that Seth really was clueless.

But he had proof otherwise. Dipping his hand in the right front pocket of his jeans, he pulled out the green marble and held it up so that it caught a shaft of light pouring into the garage from a window high above the floor.

Seth's gaze followed the movement of Sutton's hand. His eyes narrowed before his gaze dropped to meet Sutton's.

"What's your game, Seth? Why leave this for me?"

Seth remained silent, pinning Sutton with his unnerving stare.

"Thanks for the marble. I've kind of missed it." Sutton pocketed the marble and started to walk away.

"Wait," Seth said, his voice tense.

Sutton turned slowly to face the other man, waiting silently.

"April Billings worked here until July. Part-time internship."

"Doing what?"

"A little of everything, although her main job was helping out the bookkeeping staff."

"She quit in July?"

"Wanted a month off just to enjoy herself before going back to college in the fall." Seth's tone held a hint of sadness. But he was a good actor. Hard to know if his show of emotion was authentic.

"Why are you telling me this?"

"I hear you're looking into her murder. And since two other former Davenport employees have also turned up dead—"

"And look who works here."

Seth's expression darkened. "You're not seriously going there."

"Even serial killers sometimes start small."

"Yeah, torturing animals, not pulling cons."

"A con artist is just a sociopath who kills the soul instead of the body."

Seth shook his head. "Well, maybe that's so. And if you're looking for a serial soul killer, feel free to take me in for questioning."

"You're mistaking me for the police."

"That's right." The smile Seth shot Sutton looked more like a smirk. "You're working for the big chief Cooper down there in Alabama."

"Did you call your sister so I'd know where to find you?"

Seth smiled. "You're just full of conspiracy theories today."

"How did you know to find me at Ivy Hawkins's place?" Sutton pulled the marble from his pocket again. "I can't believe you still had this after all those years, Seth. Never took you for the sentimental type."

"Ivy Hawkins's place?" Seth looked surprised. Sutton didn't buy it for a second. "You're in town a day and you're already shacking up? And with the police, of all people."

"Who told you I was back in Bitterwood?"

Seth laughed, giving up the pretense. "A Calhoun can't come back to Bitterwood without the whole damn county hearing about it, Sutton. You should know that."

"Why'd you leave this marble for me at Ivy Hawkins's place?"

Seth didn't answer.

"It was you outside her house last night. What did you do, follow us from the motel? Or were you out there at Clingmans Dome?"

Seth's neutral expression slipped a moment, betraying a hint of confusion in his green eyes. "I don't know what you're talking about."

"Which part? The motel? Or the mountain?"

"I went looking for you at the motel," he said finally. "You know, for old times' sake. Saw you with the little lady cop so I decided to bide my time before making contact." His drawl broadened. "Don't know if you know this, Sutton, but I'm not real popular with the police around these parts."

"You couldn't wait until morning to get in touch with me?"

Seth's mouth curved slightly. "I figured you wouldn't care to see me if it wasn't your own idea."

"So you set me up to come looking for you?"

"And it worked."

Seth Hammond always had been too damned wily for his own good. If he'd just use some of his native intelligence for good reasons instead of bad, no telling what he could accomplish.

"What do you really want, Seth?"

"I told you what I wanted. I told you about April Billings."

"So three of the four women killed worked here in the past few years. Thanks for sharing."

"Don't you think that's strange?" Seth asked. "Three dead women who worked at the same place? Wouldn't you call that a significant connection between the victims?"

"You seem awfully interested in this case."

Seth looked injured. Sutton wasn't sure if the expression was real or carefully calculated. With Seth, you never knew. "People around here are wondering if someone's targeting the Davenports. Folks are worried about working here, especially the women."

"Are they right?" Sutton asked carefully. "Should people be worried about working here?"

"I don't know," Seth answered. "But I'd sure like to find out."

"I'D HAVE TO GO THROUGH all of our files to be sure, but I don't remember anyone here ever renting a truck to Marjorie Kenner." George Davenport looked at Ivy with apology in his blue eyes. He started walking toward the front door, leaving her little choice but to follow.

"Will you check for me?" she asked, trying to keep her tone polite and friendly rather than commanding, not so much because she thought honey would get her further than vinegar but because he looked too tired and wan to make forcefulness seem wise.

If she had to guess, she'd say Mr. Davenport was chronically ill these days. He had the thin, sallow look of someone who had lost a significant amount of weight in a short span of time. Heart trouble? Cancer? Either was possible, she supposed. He wasn't well, but to his credit, he walked at a brisk enough pace that she had to move at a clip to keep up.

"I'll check," he agreed, shielding his eyes with one hand as a truck turned into the parking lot and swung around to one side of the lot, where there was a large open bay with a large tank, a hose and what looked like a large manhole. As they both watched, the driver pulled up in front of the manhole and got out of the truck. He circled to the back and bent to pull up the manhole cover. The cover must not have been heavy, since he lifted it with little trouble and set it aside.

Turning to the truck, he opened the back doors wide and stepped back quickly. Muddy water spilled out of the back of the truck, and Ivy realized the bay was built at a slight incline to tilt downward toward the drain.

Mr. Davenport must have noticed her interest. "That's our cleaning bay. We get farmers who rent trucks to take chickens and pigs to the butcher, and folks like Stan Thomas there who rent trucks to carry live fish in aerated tanks to restaurants that want their fish to be as fresh as possible. Those kinds of transport jobs can get messy, and I've found that everyone benefits if we offer a discount to the renters to muck out the trucks themselves before we do the final sanitation."

If the muddy water were red instead of brown, Ivy thought, it would be easy to imagine the back of the truck as the scene of a bloody murder. "Do you supervise the initial cleanings?" she asked.

"No. We don't have the time or personnel for that. And if our cleaners go in and we can document that the renter did a slapdash job, we'll cut the amount of the discount. Renters know that, so they usually do a good job."

"Is the lot open at night?"

Davenport slanted a curious look at her. "The warehouse is locked up tight, but no, we don't lock up the parking area or the cleaning bay."

"So, theoretically, anyone could clean out their truck after hours?"

"Well, not anyone. You could drain stuff out, I suppose, but the only way you can get the washing equipment to work is to have the keycard for the water unit." Davenport nodded toward Stan Thomas, who had just pulled something from his pocket and ran it down a slot set into the side of the large tank. He pressed a trigger on the hose nozzle and water shot out and hit the inside of the truck with a thump. "You turn in the keycard with the truck. The water can be heated to a high enough temperature to meet sanitation requirements."

"Do you have video surveillance on the parking lot?"

"Right around the buildings, yes."

"Not the entrance or the cleaning bay?"

"No. We park the vehicles in the big garages at night, and that's locked up and protected by alarms. There's nothing in the parking lot worth bothering, and we've never had a problem with random after-hours washing." Davenport shot her a wan smile. "Are you asking for a particular reason?"

"I'm not sure," she admitted, watching the murky water running out of the back of the rented truck. "Would it be possible to get a copy of all your rental agreements for the past five months?"

Davenport frowned. "That seems unnecessarily intrusive, Detective."

"I could arrange for a warrant," she said, although she wasn't entirely sure that was true, especially since she wasn't even in her own jurisdiction.

"Then that's what I would suggest you do," Davenport said firmly. He smiled again to soften his words. "I don't mean to be difficult."

"No, I understand," she assured him, and she did. People had a right to privacy, even in a murder investigation. She'd try to get what she wanted going the legal route and hope she could make a Blount County lawman see things her way. She'd need local law enforcement to get a warrant.

"If you come across anything strange or remember anything you care to share, I can be reached at this number." She handed him one of her cards. "Thank you for your help." She watched George Davenport head back to the office, wincing as she saw his legs seem to buckle a little more with every step. Definitely ill, she thought. Should he even be at work?

As she started toward the department-issued Ford sedan she'd driven to Maryville, she looked for Sutton's truck. It wasn't parked anywhere in the lot. Of course, she hadn't noticed it when she came in, too focused on the questions she'd wanted to ask.

She pulled out her cell phone and dialed his number. He answered on the first ring. "Hey, Ivy."

Damn, but even his voice could send shivers down her back. "I thought we were going to J.T.'s Barbecue for lunch."

"Yeah, about that—I've had something come up. Rain check?"

"Will I see you back at the house tonight, or are you going to find somewhere else to stay?" She hoped the question didn't sound needy.

"I'm not sure. I'll call to let you know. I'll have to get my things from your place if I stay somewhere else anyway."

Nice and noncommittal. Hell, she should be glad if he had decided to put a little distance between them. The sooner Sutton Calhoun moseyed off to wherever he'd come from, the sooner she could go back to being a sensible cop instead of a flutter-headed idiot.

Unfortunately, the Maryville police captain to whom she outlined her case disagreed there was enough probable cause to approach a judge for a warrant. "You have a hunch, not evidence. Get me evidence and we'll talk again."

So she ended up driving back to Bitterwood in time to run into Captain Rayburn heading out to lunch, accompanied by a silver-haired man dressed in a dark blue suit. She recognized the man as the Sevier County Sheriff's Department's deputy chief of operations. They were both smiling as they came out of the building, but Rayburn took one look at her and his expression went from cheerful to thunderous. "Hawkins, I want to see you in my office when I get back."

"Yes, sir." She gave a crisp nod and moved out of his way before he and his companion bowled her over heading down the concrete steps to the personnel parking lot. She watched the two men walking away, noting that the silver-haired man was still grinning but her captain's back was as rigid as a steel girder. She released a sigh. Her day was turning out to be one giant barrel of horse manure.

Antoine Parsons caught her up on what she'd missed while she was in Maryville. "Apparently Rayburn and the chief deputy are old fishing buddies from way back. Tommy Logan dropped by to take Rayburn to lunch but mostly, I think, to give him a few friendly whacks about one of his investigators getting herself caught in a shootout up on Clingmans Dome in the middle of the night." Parsons sent a pointed look her way. "Which, by the way, you didn't think that was something worth telling your old buddy Antoine?"

He was smiling, but she heard a tone of offense beneath Parsons's light tone. She dropped heavily into her desk seat.

Yup, a big ol' barrel of manure.

THE ONE-STORY clapboard house on Kettle Creek Road hadn't changed much in fourteen years, Sutton saw. Still shabby, the sun-faded white paint job nearly flaked away by time, leaving weathered gray pine showing in scabrous patches. Just looking at the place made his gut tighten with dread.

But he wasn't eighteen anymore. He hadn't come back to get in touch with his past or anything sentimental like that.

He'd come here for answers.

At the top of the cinder-block steps to the rickety front

porch, he paused, wondering if the sagging wood slats of the porch floor would hold his weight. They creaked but didn't snap as he crossed to the ripped screen door that hung by one precarious screw from its hinges. It made a loud groan as he opened it, killing any hope he might have had for a stealthy entrance.

It didn't matter. He knew who was inside, and he didn't need sneaky ninja skills to get to the bottom of what was going on.

The front door was unlocked. Not that it would have mattered either way—Sutton knew where to find the spare key.

Some things never changed.

The living room just inside the front door was tidier than Sutton had expected. The old man had never cared much about what the place looked like; he'd saved his concern for first impressions for himself, making sure to wear nice clothes, shave and keep his hair neatly cut. He was selling an image, after all. People had to think they could trust him.

Footsteps sounded on the hardwood floor of the hallway beyond the door on the other side of the living room. Sutton steeled himself for his first glimpse of the old man in over a decade.

But it wasn't his father who walked through the door. It was the man who'd led him here today. Seth Hammond paused in the doorway, folding his arms over his chest as if to block the way. "Thought you weren't interested in a family reunion."

"Yeah, well, you're not family, so what do you know?" Sutton pushed forward, daring Seth to hold his ground.

For a moment, it seemed as if they might come to blows. Then Seth backed away, making an exaggerated gesture toward the bedroom down the hall. Sutton pushed past him, his shoulder bumping hard against Seth's, knocking the smaller man backward into the wall.

He didn't know what he'd expected to find when he finally saw his father again after so many years. An older man, his handsome face a little more lined, his dark hair liberally lined with silver.

Anything but the wheelchair-bound shell of a man who sat hunched and bitter beside the bedroom window, one hand curled into a gnarled claw and both legs thin and atrophied beneath his saggy blue jeans.

"What's wrong with him?" he asked quietly as Seth entered the room.

Seth's voice was gentle, tinged with unexpected sympathy. "Five years ago, he suffered a massive stroke. He hasn't walked or talked since."

Chapter Eight

"Did I not tell you to keep clear of Sutton Calhoun?" Glen Rayburn had a way of speaking to the officers under his command as if they were stupid, rebellious children, Ivy thought, chafing at his tone. Perhaps she deserved a dressing-down for violating the spirit if not the letter of the captain's order, but there was no call to treat her like a teenager who'd broken curfew.

"You told Mr. Calhoun not to try to involve any of us in his investigation. He didn't. I was the one who tailed him last night."

Rayburn's face reddened. "Why the hell would you do that?"

"His interest in the case interests me," she answered honestly. "We've been chasing our tails for four murders now, looking for evidence that can't be found, trying to come up with theories that make sense." She didn't add that some of their problems stemmed from Rayburn's own stubborn refusal to consider linking the murders together. It put them behind on the investigation by the time the second murder was a few hours old.

"And you think Calhoun's going to give you answers?"

"I think a fresh set of eyes can be beneficial," she answered carefully.

"Perhaps I should remove your eyes from the case altogether."

She couldn't tell if he was bluffing. "Sir, that would only put the investigation that much further behind. You'd have to bring a new detective up to speed."

"I can't have you gallivanting all over the Smoky Mountains, getting yourself shot at and making this department look like a clown act to our fellow law enforcement agencies."

A clown act? She bristled, trying not to show it. "Sir, someone deliberately targeted Sutton Calhoun for murder. He could have just as easily succeeded as failed last night."

"Didn't happen in our jurisdiction."

"It happened to me," she snapped back, clamping her lips closed to get her mouth under control. "I believe it's connected."

"I don't see it," Rayburn disagreed.

She tried changing directions. "Mr. Calhoun and I are not collaborating on the murder investigation." Well, not directly. She'd probably shared a little more information with him last night while waiting for the cops than she should have, but it didn't really seem to be much he didn't know already.

"And yet, he's staying at your house, isn't he?"

She stared back at the captain, wondering how on earth he knew that.

"After my visit with Deputy Chief Logan I made a call to the motel where Calhoun was staying. The office said he'd checked out last night and left with you."

Small-town grapevine, she thought bleakly. Faster than a bullet.

"You going to tell me he slept on your sofa?"

Her gaze, which had started to wander, snapped back to meet his, appalled by his insinuation. "Sir, my personal life, insofar as it does not affect my work, is not anyone else's business."

"Personal life?" Rayburn's tone edged toward sleazy. She darkened her expression, and he seemed to realize he'd crossed a line. "You're right. I can't police your personal life if you're breaking no laws. But don't forget that you have an obligation to protect the integrity of this investigation."

"Yes, sir."

"Very well. Dismissed."

She walked stiffly back to the investigators' bull pen, ignoring Antoine's curious gaze as she dropped into her desk chair and started riffling through her messages. Mostly junk, except a follow-up call from the medical examiner who'd done the autopsy on Marjorie Kenner earlier that morning. He wanted to discuss the results. "You didn't take the call from Shelton?"

"I was out on a witness call. Does he have the autopsy results?"

"Yeah." She finished going through the notes. Nothing from Sutton. "I'll give Shelton a call."

The medical examiner, Carl Shelton, worked for the regional forensic center at the University of Tennessee Medical Center in Knoxville. He was out to lunch when she called, so she left a message.

"Where've you been all morning?" Antoine asked when she hung up.

She told him about her visit to Davenport Trucking. "They rent trucks out to farmers to transport livestock to the butcher and butchers to transport meat to the packing plant. I watched a guy cleaning out the back of the truck just today. It almost looked like he'd killed someone in there." She looked at Antoine, willing him to make the same connection she had.

His dark eyes widened. "Oh, my God."

"So I'm not crazy?"

"We need to get our hands on a list of renters."

"Davenport won't supply it without a warrant. I made a case to one of the Maryville LEOs, but he said we didn't have enough probable cause to apply for a warrant."

"For mercy's sake, do we have to supply a truck with body parts in it?"

"I hope not."

"It would explain everything." Antoine sat back in his desk chair, rubbing his chin. "Why there's no blood evidence around the bodies."

"He washes them down inside the truck." Ivy tamped down a shudder at the image flickering in her head. "Removes trace evidence, gets rid of the spilled blood—"

"Then transports the clean body back to her home." Antoine shook his head. "Why do it that way, though? Just to get rid of the evidence?"

"If we could find the truck or trucks he's used, we could probably find trace evidence."

"What about the drain at the trucking company?"

"Apparently there are trucks going in and out of that cleaning bay daily. Anything that might have gone down the drain the night of Marjorie Kenner's murder has washed away already."

"There's got to be some way we can test out this theory."

"Unfortunately, I can't think of anything short of a warrant, which we can't get yet, or waiting for the next murder, which I sure as hell don't want to do." Ivy rubbed her temples, where a frustration headache was beginning to set up shop and make a racket. She'd skipped lunch after a hasty breakfast of instant oatmeal. Why she hadn't stopped for barbecue without Sutton, she didn't know. Or maybe she knew but just didn't want to think about how pathetic she was acting where he was concerned.

She checked her cell phone to see if she'd missed a call from Sutton while she was talking to Captain Rayburn. No messages.

He'd seemed preoccupied when they'd parted ways at the trucking company. Had he seen the truck in the cleaning bay and come to the same conclusion she had?

If so, what was he up to now?

SETH HAMMOND WALKED past Sutton, who stood frozen and numb in the middle of his father's bedroom. Setting a tray of food on the table next to Cleve's wheelchair, Seth stuck a straw in a glass of iced tea and shifted the fork to the left side of the plate.

"Made your favorite," he told the chair-bound man, whose expression softened as he looked up at the younger man. "Chicken bites with honey mustard dip. And this time, you eat those carrot sticks I cut up for you instead of throwing them at the TV."

Seth looked at Sutton. "Cleve likes to watch Judge Everett, but he gets a little too involved and ends up throwing things at the litigants." He grinned at Cleve. "Always the vegetables, I notice, Cleveland. You're not foolin' me, you old coot."

Cleve made a grunting sound and waved his good hand at the television.

"Hold your horses, old man. I'm getting there." Seth picked up the remote from the side table and handed it to Cleve. The older man frowned his displeasure and tried to hand it back to Seth. "No, sir, you know you're supposed to be doing things for yourself. You've got a good hand. Use it."

Sutton felt a flood of nausea rise up his throat as Cleve

growled his displeasure at Seth, but Seth just laughed it off and nodded for Sutton to follow him out of the room.

Seth closed the bedroom door behind him and headed toward the living room, nodding his head for Sutton to follow. "He knows how to use the remote. He just likes to have someone snap to attention whenever he barks."

Sutton stopped in the middle of the hallway, forcing Seth to stop and turn around. "Five years of that?"

"It was a lot worse for the first year or so. He couldn't do much for himself at all then. I know it's hard to tell, but he's made a good bit of progress. Not as much as he should've, but you know what a stubborn old cuss he can be, and the stroke made him that much worse."

"Why didn't anyone tell me?"

Seth's eyes glittered with meaning. "You wouldn't take my calls."

Damn. Seth *had* tried to call him about five years earlier, but Sutton had ignored the messages. He'd been up to his eyeballs in jihadists on a daily basis. The last thing he'd wanted to deal with was his old friend's latest mess. "I thought you wanted me to bail you out or something."

"Lucky for me I didn't," Seth murmured, gesturing toward the doorway into the living room. "Come on, let's sit down. You're looking a little pasty."

Sutton dropped into the nearest armchair, his knees feeling shaky. "God."

Seth sat on the sofa adjacent, leaning forward a little. "Seriously, you okay? You want a glass of water?"

"Did the doctors know what caused it? High blood pressure?"

Seth's lips quirked slightly, though they didn't quite make it to a smile. "I reckon Bart Ludlow would call it divine retribution."

Sutton frowned, not following.

"Remember when Ludlow filled your daddy's backside full of buckshot for messing around with Ludlow's wife?"

"Yeah."

"Well, they didn't get all the buckshot out, as you probably remember. Apparently one of those pellets did something they call 'embolize.' Went right up his bloodstream, lodged in a vessel in his head and caused a stroke."

"God." How bloody typical, he thought, that one of his father's myriad sins would have come back to bite him. "Who found him?"

"I did. I usually checked on him every day or so. Doctor said the timing was damned near a miracle. Too much longer and they couldn't have saved him."

"Did he ask to see me after he was awake?"

Seth's eyes narrowed. "I told you, he can't talk."

In other words, Sutton thought, he hadn't. Why would he? Sutton had left the second he turned eighteen and made it clear to his father that he didn't want to see him again. "He can understand you, right?"

Seth nodded. "The doctors aren't sure why he's not able to talk. They think it might be psychosomatic. You know how vain Cleve's always been about his looks. The doctors speculated staying mute might be a way to avoid interacting with other folks when he's this way."

"What about therapy? Is he still getting therapy?"

"I take him once a week. It's all he'll agree to, and he fights them all the way. I get the feeling the folks at the rehab place would be happy as pigs in slop if Cleve never came back, but I'm not ready to give up on him yet."

Sutton stared at the other man, not sure what he was feeling. Guilt, certainly, but was there also a little envy? Envy that Seth Hammond was playing the role of Cleve's son, doing the things Sutton should have been doing? "And he never asked for me?"

"I reckon he knew you wouldn't come."

"Nobody gave me the chance."

"I called—"

"You could have kept at it. Sent a letter or, hell, you could have had Delilah tell me."

"I wasn't sure it was a good idea." Seth's voice lowered a notch. "You made it real clear you weren't coming back here and Cleve was a big reason why. I wasn't sure draggin' you back here kicking and screaming would have been any good for him. He needs somebody who actually gives a damn, not somebody who feels guilty and obligated."

Sutton wanted to argue. He wanted to slap that mildly scolding look off Seth Hammond's face and tell him to get the hell out of his house. But it wasn't his house. And apparently, for the past five years, at least, Seth had been a far better son to Cleve than Sutton ever had.

"I know he didn't show it, but I think he was real glad to see you."

The only thing worse than Seth's disapproval was his compassionate pity. "Give me a break. I saw how he looked at me."

"Why did you come here today, Sutton?"

Sutton thought about lying, but he realized the truth might get him a lot further with Seth. Like a lot of con men, Seth was as good at spotting a lie as he was at telling one. "I was following you."

Seth's eyebrows notched upward a moment before his expression went neutral. "Should I be flattered or take out a restraining order?"

Sutton didn't answer.

"It's about the murders, right?"

"You work at a place where three of the four victims worked."

"So, naturally, I'm the prime suspect."

Sutton wished he could say yes, just to wipe the annoyed look off Seth's face. What did he expect? He'd happily followed in Cleve's scam-pulling footsteps, taking to the confidence game as if he was born for it. "Your hands aren't the cleanest in the county."

"I haven't pulled a con in years. And I've never been violent. You know that." Seth smirked. "I'm a lover, not a fighter."

"You're awfully interested in the murders. I mean, you went to a lot of trouble to get in contact with me about what you knew."

"Mr. Davenport hired me when a whole lot of people wouldn't have let me in the door. He took a chance on me, and if I can do anything to protect him and his business—"

"Sounds personal."

"Like I said, he took a chance. Not many would've."

"Did you hear there was another murder yesterday?"

Seth looked at him as if he'd lost his mind. "I knew about it before lunchtime. You know how this town is."

"Did Marjorie Kenner ever work at Davenport Trucking?"

"No, as far as I know, she retired from the school and took to tutoring out of her house to make a little pocket change."

"Could there be any connection between her and anyone at the company? Maybe she rented a truck?"

"I don't think so." Seth's brow furrowed. "I've been working there a little over a year, so she might have done it before my time. But why would a serial killer target someone who just rented a truck?"

Damned good question, Sutton had to concede. April Billings had been twenty years old. Marjorie Kenner had to be in her late fifties at the very youngest. "Did you know either of the other two women who died?" he asked Seth.

"Amelia Sanderson I knew. She worked in the office until her death. I also knew Coral Vines from growing up, remember? Ah, maybe you didn't. She was younger than us and by the time she came to high school, you were already halfway out of town. The women at the office talked about her all the time. Apparently she went off the deep end straight into a bottle after her husband got killed in combat in Afghanistan." Seth's eyes narrowed slightly as he lifted his gaze to meet Sutton's, a hint of awareness in his green eyes. He would know that Sutton had joined the army. That it was likely he'd traveled overseas, to Iraq or Afghanistan or any number of hot spots where the United States had stationed forces.

But Sutton didn't want his admiration or pity or whatever it was those sharp green eyes were trying to say to him. "How old were they?"

The question seemed to surprise Seth. "Um, I don't know about Amelia—probably around our age. Maybe a year or two younger. She lived in Bitterwood. Everybody who's been killed so far did, even though they're working in Maryville."

That was interesting, too, Sutton thought. "And Coral Vines?"

"Late twenties. She was three years behind us in school."

So Marjorie Kenner was the outlier. Interesting.

There was a clattering noise from the back of the house. Seth jumped to action, beating Sutton to his father's bedroom by a couple of steps.

The remote control lay on the floor in front of the television, the plastic casing holding the batteries popped open and the batteries lying a few feet away, still rolling.

Cleve made an odd grunting noise, waving his good hand at his empty plate. Seth started laughing as he bent to pick up the remote. Sutton saw his father was smiling, too, looking almost like his old, charming self.

"He'd already eaten the carrots," Seth explained. "So when it came time to throw something at the litigants—"

"Never were good at impulse control, were you, Cleve?" Sutton stopped one of the rolling batteries with his foot and bent to pick it up. He crossed to sit on the bed beside his father. "I know you think you have all the answers, old man. But you can do better than this." He waved his hand at his father's wheelchair. "Maybe you'll never be what you were before. But maybe that's good, you ever think of that?"

Seth cleared his throat but didn't say anything.

"I get the feeling you only respond to tough love, so I'm going to lay a little on you here." Sutton put his hand on the arm of the wheelchair. "You never were much for a boy to be proud of. You made your living by tricking people out of their hard-earned money, and you never seemed to have a bit of remorse about doing it. So maybe you ought to look at this as God's way of slapping you upside the head and telling you to do better."

Cleve's eyes flashed with anger, but he didn't look away.

"Seth tells me he's gone legit. And it didn't take a stroke to do it." He gave the wheelchair arm a little shake, making his father's body shake with it. "He also tells me you aren't doing what the therapists are telling you to do to get better. Is that another scam? You've figured out how to get the government to support you for the rest of your life without your having to lift a finger?"

"Sutton—"

Cleve growled something that sounded oddly like the word "rich." Sutton looked at Seth for interpretation and found Seth staring at Cleve, a look of surprise and delight on his face.

"You old coot! You *can* talk if you put your mind to

it." He slanted a look at Sutton. "Or if someone pisses you off enough."

"What did he mean by 'rich'?"

"I believe what he was telling you was that he doesn't need the government—or you—takin' care of him," Seth answered with half a smile. "He was good at more than just convincing otherwise smart people to hand money to him, you see. He was also good at investing."

Sutton looked from Seth to his father. Cleve gazed back at him, his hazel eyes, so like Sutton's own, glittering with triumph. "How much?"

"About five million, give or take a few hundred thousand."

Sutton stared in shocked dismay. "Ill-gotten gains, you old bastard."

Cleve looked unrepentant.

"I'm not sure it's all ill-gotten," Seth said quietly. "Some of the things your daddy did weren't exactly illegal."

"Just immoral."

"No doubt. But there's millionaires all over the world you could say that about." Seth held out his hand for the battery Sutton had picked up. Sutton handed it over and Seth reassembled the remote. He passed it back to Cleve. "You don't have to like it, Sutton. It just is what it is. The feds and the local cops know about it and can't make a legal claim to take it away from him. And since it keeps him from sucking the government coffers dry, nobody's raising much of a stink."

"Who's administering his money?"

"I am." Seth met Sutton's gaze without flinching.

"Convenient."

Cleve grumbled something that sounded profane. Seth's lips twitched.

"I guess you've got everything under control, then, don't

you, Seth?" The urge to get out of there, to leave the toxic past and confounding present behind him, was more than Sutton could resist. "I wanted to know what you were up to. I guess now I do." He turned and walked out of the room, wishing he had never come here.

Seth caught up with him at the front door. "Wait."

Sutton whipped around to face him, his fists clenching with a rush of unexpected rage. "What?"

"There's one other thing I was pondering telling you, but I didn't want you to get the wrong impression. But since you clearly can't think any less of me than you already do, what the hell? A month ago, an acquaintance of mine approached me outside a bar in Maryville to ask me if I wanted to make a quick twenty grand."

Sutton frowned, not sure where Seth was going with this story. "And?"

"Turns out, he wanted me to kill someone."

Chapter Nine

"We may have a chance at a warrant."

Ivy nearly ran off on the shoulder as she left the main highway onto Vesper Road. "You're kidding."

Antoine's voice sounded jubilant over the cell phone's hands-free speaker. "I have a friend on the Maryville force. Seems he's got the chief's ear, and once I told him about the cases and why we think Davenport Trucking might be peripherally involved, he convinced the chief to call a judge friend of his. He's supposed to call me back in the morning with the judge's response. He's asking for a list of names covering rentals from two weeks before the first murder to the present—that should be all we need, don't you think?"

It was better than she'd hoped for when she left the office with Antoine still making calls. "It should be."

"He's not going to bother the judge before morning, so go home and get some rest. You look like hell."

"You're such a flatterer, Antoine."

She pushed the call end button and slowed as she approached the turn into her driveway. To her surprise, Sutton's truck was parked next to the house. Since she hadn't heard from him since leaving Davenport Trucking, she'd figured he'd found somewhere else to stay for the night.

He was sitting on her front porch, a six-pack of Corona beer on the step beside him. Only one was missing from the pack, she saw as she walked slowly up the path to the steps. It dangled from the fingers of his left hand, still half-full. So unless he'd already been through another six-pack, at least he wasn't drunk.

But he looked as if he wanted to be.

"You didn't call," she murmured as he lifted his smoldering gaze to meet hers.

"I wasn't sure I was going to come back here."

"But here you are."

He lifted the bottle to his mouth and took a swig. "Yeah. Here I am."

She dropped onto the porch step next to him. He reached into the six-pack and brought out a bottle. "Want one?"

She was tempted, but she had a feeling at least one of them should stay completely sober tonight. "No, thanks."

He shrugged and put the bottle down beside him. "I saw my father."

"Yeah?"

"Why didn't you warn me he'd had a stroke?"

His words gave her a start. "You didn't know?"

Haunted eyes lifted to meet hers. "No."

"I figured you knew." She had seen Cleve Calhoun only a couple of times since his stroke, once at a Knoxville hospital when she was there to check on an assault victim and, more recently, when Seth Hammond had taken him to the local clinic for his flu shot while she was there getting a sprained ankle treated. Seeing Cleve Calhoun, one of the most alive men she'd ever encountered, wheelchair bound and mute had come as a jolt to her system. "You must have been really shocked to see him that way."

He took another drink. "Understatement."

"Nobody tried to contact you when he had the stroke?" If she'd had any idea he'd been left in the dark, she'd have tried to track him down herself.

"Seth did, but I didn't take his calls." He sounded bitter, but she had a feeling he was blaming himself more than Seth.

"Still, he should have kept trying to contact you."

Sutton paused with the beer bottle halfway to his mouth. "I didn't exactly give him any reason to think I cared."

"Of course you care. He's your father." As frustrated as she could get with her mother's foolish choices, Ivy still loved her and wanted the best for her. And she knew how hard Sutton had struggled with his conflicted feelings back when they were little more than kids. "How is he?"

"Stubborn. Foolish." Sutton put the bottle down beside him and put his head in his hands, his elbows propped on his knees. "I don't even know what I feel, to tell you the truth. Horrified to see him that way? Relieved that he's Seth's problem and not mine?"

"Sutton—"

"I'm a real piece of work, aren't I?" He looked up at the rising moon, his face bathed in cool light. He was smiling, but there was no humor in the expression, making it look like a twisted grimace. "Relieved that I don't have to deal with my cripple of a father."

"Your feelings about him are complicated. They always have been—"

"Stop it!" He whipped his head around to look at her, making her flinch. "Stop trying to justify my selfishness."

She pressed her lips flat, anger flaring in her chest. She pushed to her feet. "Fine. Drink yourself stupid. I'm going inside."

"Wait." He reached out and caught her leg, his hand closing around her calf. Heat burned through the fabric of her cotton trousers to brand her flesh.

His fingers slid slowly upward, making her heart skip a beat.

"I'm sorry." His voice was a caress. "I didn't mean to snap."

Oh, God. His fingers had stopped climbing, but they hadn't stopped moving, drawing circles across the crease behind her knee. He looked up at her, his eyes combustive. She felt her body catch fire in response, heat flooding her from her breasts to her sex.

"Sutton—"

He rose to his feet with unexpected grace, lithe and sinuous like a cat on the prowl. Suddenly he was towering over her, his face cast in half shadow. Moonlight bathed the other side of his face, painting him in cool blue tones like a sculpture.

His hand trailed up her arm, his calloused fingers seeming to shoot sparks along her nerve endings. "I look at you," he murmured in a low tone, "and I still see a shadow of that dark-eyed kid who used to watch me when she thought I wasn't looking. I wonder now, what were you thinking?"

She couldn't tell him that she'd thought he was the most beautiful thing she'd ever seen, a wild buck kicking against the constraints of his small-town captivity. Part of her had known he'd have to run free, sooner or later, but another part had prayed he'd grow content with his confinement, so she would never have to see him go.

"My mama told me you were nothing but trouble," she said, her voice coming out in a hoarse whisper. "She always said, 'Calhouns will break your heart.'"

He looked thoughtful. "Do you think she knew from experience?"

"Your daddy always was a charming old cuss, and you know how my mama is. Always looking for something."

He brushed away a piece of hair that had fallen out of her ponytail and into her face, tucking it behind her ear.

"I'm not drunk, Ivy." His finger trailed along the curve of her jaw, making her shiver. "I just want you to know that."

She had trouble finding her voice. "Why's that?"

He bent toward her. "Because I'm going to kiss you now," he whispered, sending her sluggish brain into a tailspin. Before she could regain her equilibrium, his mouth was hot and soft against hers, more seductive than demanding. But the effect was the same—fire raging out of control in her blood, molten heat pooling low in her belly and every nerve ending in her body on alert, aching for the brush of his skin against hers.

Not even in her most vivid adolescent dreams had she imagined how easily she could be conquered by his touch. No last-ditch effort to keep her head, no defiant last stand, just complete, eager surrender. When he snaked his arms around her waist, tugging her flush to his hard body, she melted into him, her hands driving through his crisp, dark hair to pull him even closer.

He tasted like Corona and sex, his tongue sliding over hers, demanding a response. She gave it to him, moving her hands under the hem of his T-shirt until her fingertips dug into the heated velvet of his back. She traced the valleys and ridges of his muscles, thrilling at the sound of his low groan in response. She wasn't sure when or how they moved, but suddenly her back flattened against the rough clapboard wall next to the front door and Sutton grabbed her hips, lifting her until she was pinned against the front of her house, her thighs cradling his narrow hips.

The ridge of his erection pressed into her through the layers of cotton and denim that stood between them, teasing her sex until a long, fierce shudder rocked through her.

"I want you," he breathed against her throat just before he nipped at the tendon, making her moan.

She wanted him, too. More than she'd thought was possible. Far more than was wise. She put her hands between their bodies and stroked him boldly through his jeans, satisfaction swamping her as he released a helpless groan. "You like that?"

He caught her hand and twined his fingers with hers, guiding her hand away from his erection. "Slow down. Let's just slow this down."

She didn't want slow. She wanted fast and fierce, so she didn't have time to think. "Don't give me a chance—"

He drew his head back so he could look into her eyes. His hands, well on their way to a thorough examination of the curves of her breast, went still, leaving her restless with need. "Don't give you a chance to what?"

She shook her head, reaching for his belt. "Doesn't matter."

He caught her hands, stopping her. "A chance to say no?"

She felt the change in him, the sudden return of control. Steel in his backbone, determination glittering in his eyes—he was no longer an animal caught up in the thrall of lust but a man with complete mastery of even his most primal desires.

Damn it.

She pulled her hands away from him and slid away, finding her unsteady feet. "I don't want to say no."

"But you should?"

She leaned against the frame of the front door, pressing her forehead to the cool wood. "Sex complicates everything."

He didn't argue. "I'll find somewhere else to stay."

She shook her head. "No." At his pained look, she added, "At least, not until I talk to you about something."

ONE OF THE MOST USEFUL things his time in the Army Special Forces had taught Sutton was how to control himself in any situation. Granted, his steely mastery of his body usually translated to remaining utterly still in the most uncomfortable of positions and locations in order to get the advantage over an enemy. But he'd also learned how to discipline his other, more primal urges.

Unfortunately, not even a decade in the Special Forces had equipped him to control the hunger to finish what he and Ivy had started on her front porch.

Once inside, she'd kept a careful distance from him, puttering around the kitchen while he waited at the breakfast nook table for her to finish putting together sandwiches for their dinner. He'd offered to help but she'd warned him off with a desperate look and a wave of her hands, so he'd settled at the table and kept his hands to himself.

As she passed the phone on the counter, she put down the plates and checked her messages. Sutton heard her mother's voice on the recorder. "Birdy, give me a call. I need to talk to you about something." Ivy erased the message and picked up the plates again.

He smiled at her mother's use of the nickname "Birdy." "She still calls you Birdy?"

"Yeah." She smiled, though there was a hint of a grimace in it. "And Antoine calls me Hawk, did you notice that? I'm apparently destined for bird-related nicknames."

He supposed "Birdy" had fit her when she was a small, brown, quiet little thing, but he agreed with Antoine on this one. She was more raptor than wren these days.

"Don't you need to call her back?" he asked as she set his sandwich in front of him, making no move toward the phone.

"I'll call her later." She sat down across from him.

"So, what did you want to tell me?"

She pushed her sandwich around the paper plate. "When I was at Davenport today, I saw something interesting."

She told him about the truck in the self-cleaning bay and how she thought it might connect to the murders.

Even a discussion of mobile abattoirs couldn't cool his lust completely, but at least it gave his one-track mind a detour to work through. "You think the killer's using a rented truck as his own personal butcher's shop?"

Ivy looked at him briefly, little more than a glancing blow of her gaze before she looked away. "We're hoping we'll get a warrant in the morning and then we can start questioning people."

"I have some news for you, too." He paused, he realized with a hint of guilt, because he knew it would force her to look at him again. He missed having that brown-eyed gaze lock with his, all serious intensity and singular focus. He was beginning to kick himself for being noble instead of selfish. If he'd kept his mouth shut, he'd probably be buried inside her right now, having the best sex of his whole damned life.

It would have been amazing. He could tell that from the fireworks going off inside him with the slightest brush of her fingers on his skin. And they had history, too, a connection that even fourteen years apart hadn't been able to completely sever.

She turned her gaze toward him, a slow, wary sidelong glance that lingered when he remained silent. She finally broke the quiet standoff with an impatient "What?"

"Somebody tried to hire Seth Hammond for a contract murder."

Her mouth formed a silent O.

"Yeah, that was about my reaction, too."

"Who?"

"He wouldn't tell me. He says the guy was a middleman, tried to subcontract him to do the killing and split the money with him. Seth says he's positive the other guy chickened out and he doesn't want to sic the cops on him for making a dumb mistake."

"Seth's sympathy for the criminal element is touching." Her tone was flat and dry.

"I asked if the guy knew who'd tried to hire him. Apparently the contact was all done by phone, and the guy who tried to subcontract never got a name. And he didn't recognize the voice."

"Odd." She looked away and asked, "What makes you think any of this is connected to the murders?"

"The timing, for one. Seth said the man approached him about three weeks before the first murder."

"But how does that track with the style of these murders? These don't look like contract killings."

"Seth was told he should make them look like accidents or something else, anything but a hit."

She stopped with her sandwich halfway to her mouth. "Really."

"I was thinking, making them look like serial murders might be a way to throw the cops off what was really going on."

She finished taking a bite of sandwich, chewing slowly, a thoughtful look on her face.

He was officially in serious trouble, he thought, watching her eat and feeling the slow, steady burn of desire roiling just under the fragile surface of his control. If he couldn't get his mind off sex while watching her chew a turkey sandwich and talk about serial murders—

"Let's say this theory is right." She set her half-eaten sandwich on her plate and looked at him with such intensity he felt the lid on his libido rattling from the pressure. "If these four victims were hired murders, who wanted them dead? And why?"

He took a drink of beer to wash down a bite of sandwich. "I've been thinking about that ever since Seth told me what he knew. Finding that answer isn't really that much different than figuring out who a serial killer might be, is it? It's all about the victim."

"And two of the four worked at Davenport Trucking."

"Actually, three," Sutton corrected. "April Billings worked there part-time shortly before she was murdered."

"Are you sure?"

"That's what Seth Hammond said."

"Hmm. Mr. Davenport didn't mention that. Of course, I didn't ask. I got sidetracked by seeing the truck being cleaned out in the washing bay."

"So three of the four are connected to the trucking company."

"Marjorie Kenner's body was released by the medical examiner this afternoon. The funeral is tomorrow afternoon." Ivy's brow creased in thought. "The day of the murder, Antoine and I canvassed the whole area looking for any potential witnesses, but her house is so far from any of her neighbors, we had no luck. And all of them swear there's nobody in the world who'd want her dead."

"But if it was a contract killing, maybe the motive isn't obvious."

"Right. Maybe we've been asking all the wrong questions."

SUTTON AND HIS SIX-PACK of Corona had left soon after dinner. Ivy knew she should have been glad to see him go, along with the reckless temptation he posed, but the house felt empty with him gone. Which was stupid, since she'd lived happily alone since she was twenty-two years old, with absolutely no desire to have her peaceful existence invaded by another human being.

But she'd never considered the possibility that Sutton

Calhoun might come back to Bitterwood. He'd always been a game changer for her.

He couldn't tell her where he planned to stay, and she wasn't sure he hadn't just parked off the side of the road and spent the night in his truck, but when she arrived at Padgett Memorial Gardens for Marjorie Kenner's funeral the next morning, Sutton was there already, looking freshly showered and shaved and wearing an appropriately conservative charcoal suit and black tie.

He caught her eye as she entered the cemetery chapel, and she slid onto the pew beside him. "Where'd you find to stay?"

"Maisey Ledbetter took pity on me and gave me a room over the diner." He smiled slightly. "Free biscuits and gravy for breakfast."

"And they say your *daddy* is the con man," she murmured, slanting a look at him.

"Any word on the warrant yet?"

Ugh. She'd almost forgotten. "Apparently the judge didn't think our conjecture constituted probable cause." Antoine had called her early that morning with the bad news. "He's willing to reconsider if we can bring him something new."

"So we'll just have to find something new." He fell silent, leaving Ivy searching for something to say in response. But it was taking all her willpower, especially with his body so close, so warm and solid beside her, not to think about the night before, the way his hands had moved over her flesh, sure and possessive, as if marking her with his brand.

Apparently, his mind was traveling similar territory, for his next words came out low and seductive. "I didn't want to leave last night."

She closed her eyes against the assault on her senses. "I know."

He shook his head. "I didn't think it would be so hard. Being here in Bitterwood, I mean."

"Maybe you left more unfinished business than you realized."

He didn't answer, and the opportunity for further conversation was lost as the minister of the local Methodist church entered the chapel, signaling the beginning of the funeral service.

The crowd was larger than Ivy had anticipated, although she supposed it made sense. A combination of nostalgia—Marjorie Kenner had been a four-year fixture in the lives of any person who'd attended the local high school during her twenty-year tenure as librarian there—and morbid curiosity had probably brought most of them here.

Most of the faces were familiar, though she didn't recognize some of the mourners who sat in the pews set aside for family and close friends. She made a mental note to make contact after the graveside service and introduce herself.

Unfortunately, Captain Rayburn beat her to it. He made his way to the inner circle of mourners as soon as the graveside service was over, shooting Ivy a disapproving look as he spotted Sutton standing beside her.

"Your captain seems unhappy," Sutton murmured.

"He told me to stay away from you."

"I thought he just told you not to share investigation secrets with me."

"Yeah, well, I'm not doing so hot with that, either." She let her gaze drift across the rest of the mourners now dispersing from the cemetery. One woman in particular caught Ivy's attention, primarily because she had moved away from the rest of the crowd and now stood in front of another grave, one Ivy recognized from a previous funeral vigil only two weeks earlier.

She started moving toward the woman, her curiosity fully piqued.

Sutton fell in step with her. "What is it?"

She nodded toward the woman, who was tall and slim and dressed in a conservative blue suit. "I don't know who that is, but she just left Marjorie Kenner's funeral to visit Coral Vines's grave."

The woman looked up as they approached, her brow furrowed. Sadness darkened her red-rimmed blue eyes. "Can I help you?"

Ivy flashed her shield. "I'm Detective Hawkins with the Bitterwood Police Department. Were you a friend of Marjorie Kenner?"

"She was my neighbor when I was a little girl." Her lips curved slightly. "We bonded over a love of books and stayed in touch ever since. I can't believe she's gone."

Ivy nodded at the simple gravestone in front of the woman. "You knew Coral Vines, too?"

"Yes." The word came out in a gusty breath. "She worked for my father for a while. We became friends until—"

"Your father?" Sutton asked. "Who's your father?"

She gave him a wary look, as if she suddenly realized this was more than just a friendly conversation. "George Davenport. Coral worked at our trucking company in Maryville."

Chapter Ten

"It's been so surreal. I knew all four of the victims really well. How often does that happen?"

Her name was Rachel Davenport. Sutton supposed that, in less grief-stricken days, she'd be considered a pretty girl. She had cool blue eyes, fair skin dusted with freckles and long, straight hair the color of honey in sunlight. She was tall, towering over Ivy, but there was a fragility to her that made Sutton want to find her a chair before she collapsed.

"Not often," Ivy answered, her tone gentle, as if she, too, realized Rachel Davenport was someone with whom she had to tread lightly. "Did you know the other women through their work at your father's company?"

She nodded, her gaze lengthening, as if to take in the rest of the cemetery. "They're all here. I guess that's to be expected in a town this small, huh?"

She really did look as if she was going to fall down any moment, Sutton thought with alarm. He exchanged a look with Ivy, and she stepped forward, laying her hand on Rachel's arm. "Do you have a ride home?"

Rachel looked at Ivy as if she'd asked a strange question. "I have my car here."

Ivy glanced at Sutton again.

"I'm not going to break," Rachel said, fire in her voice.

Color rose in her cheeks, driving out the paleness. "I'm fine."

Her irritation seemed to have strengthened the steel in her spine, for she looked stronger already. Ivy took her hand away from the woman's arm and gave Sutton a shrugging look.

"I could use a cup of coffee before I get back to my normal day," he said. "Would you ladies like to join me?"

Rachel and Ivy both gave him similarly disbelieving looks, as if to ask, *Is that the best you can do?*

"Look, if you want to interrogate me or something," Rachel said, directing her words to Ivy, "just say so. I'll happily cooperate, though I'm not sure what I can add."

"I really could use a cup of coffee," Sutton said. "How about we grab a cup at Ledbetter's and you can tell us all about your friends?"

A murmured request from Ivy to Maisey Ledbetter got them a corner booth at the diner, well away from the other afternoon patrons. Ivy slid onto the booth bench next to Sutton, the heat of her body against his generating a pleasant but bearable buzz of sexual awareness. Rachel Davenport sat opposite them, her slim hands worrying the small plastic container of sugar and sweetener packets.

"I feel like a jinx," she murmured, her gaze focused on the movement of her fingers. "Everyone around me dies."

"Your father's sick, isn't he?" Ivy asked.

Sutton looked at her. She slanted a glance his way as if to ask him to back her up with whatever she said. He settled back, letting her take the lead.

"Liver cancer. Inoperable. They're hoping the chemo might give him more time, but I think he's given up hope." Rachel's lower lip trembled, but she brought it under control. Sutton realized he'd underestimated her. She looked fragile, and clearly she was struggling with a hellish amount of personal stress and grief, but she was stronger than she looked.

"What about your mother?"

"She died when I was fifteen."

Damn, Sutton thought. No wonder she felt like a jinx.

"I bet Marjorie Kenner stepped in for you then. A maternal figure in your life."

Rachel's gaze flicked upward, meeting Ivy's. "I'd never really thought of it that way, but, yeah. I guess she did."

"Amelia and Coral were around your age," Ivy said. "Did you socialize with them?"

"Amelia was my best friend from college. We bonded over our love of old movies," Rachel said with a faint smile. "We used to go to that revival theater in Knoxville on weekends when they were showing the old romantic comedies. Cary Grant, Katharine Hepburn, Irene Dunn, Myrna Loy—" She looked back at her hands. "We were supposed to go the weekend she died."

"What about Coral?" Sutton asked.

"Coral was a mess." Rachel's voice darkened with regret. "She just couldn't get past losing Derek. I tried to make sure she had something to eat and that she didn't drink herself to death. I was so afraid she'd give up and do something terrible to herself. I just never thought she'd go the way she did."

Four victims, Sutton thought. They'd thought Davenport Trucking might be the connection. But that was only half the answer.

The real connection seemed to be Rachel Davenport herself.

"Do you have any enemies?" he asked aloud.

Two sets of eyes snapped up to look at him. "Enemies?" Rachel asked, sounding confused.

Beside him, Ivy closed her hand over his knee, her grip

strong. "Of your family," she said. "Since three of the victims worked for your father."

Sutton took advantage of the situation to close his fingers over Ivy's below the table. She shot him a questioning look and he returned it with a wicked half smile.

"You think someone is killing these people because of my family?" Rachel looked horrified by the thought. "But I thought it was a serial killer or something. You think it's not?"

"I didn't say that," Ivy said quickly. "We're just trying to figure out if there could be some sort of connection in the way the killer chooses his victims. Maybe he lives close to the business, for instance. Or rents a truck from you now and then."

"We rent out a lot of trucks," Rachel said doubtfully. "Most of our customers are business owners who don't need a truck enough to warrant buying a company vehicle, though. Normal people."

Seemingly normal people could commit heinous crimes, Sutton knew. Some of the most notorious serial killers in history had struck their neighbors as perfectly normal people.

"I asked your father to let us see the rental records for the past month or so," Ivy said. "He didn't want to—privacy concerns, he said. I totally respect that, but if we knew who the renters were—"

"You think the killer could be one of our renters?"

"We think it might be," Ivy said, apparently unwilling to elaborate on their suspicions about how the rental trucks were really being used. Sutton didn't blame her. That was a lot of nightmarish speculation to lay on a civilian.

"I guess it makes sense. If he rents from us, he could have seen all of his victims there at the office," Rachel conceded. "Three of them worked there, and Marjorie often dropped by to take me to lunch when she was in town."

Sutton didn't say it aloud, but there was still something about Marjorie Kenner's murder that didn't fit. Even if she dropped by now and then to take Rachel to lunch, what were the odds that she happened to be there at the same time as a truck renter? Or that she'd catch his eye when he seemed to be more focused on women in their late twenties and early thirties?

"I'll talk to my father," Rachel said. "Make him see that we need to give you those names."

"We'll be very discreet about interviewing them," Ivy promised, a tremor of excitement underlying her calm tone.

Rachel pushed aside her coffee cup. "I'd like to go back to the cemetery now."

"Okay," Ivy agreed, glancing quickly at Sutton. He could tell she was worried she'd pushed too hard, but with Rachel's next words, she visibly relaxed.

"I'll talk to my father as soon as I get back to the office. If I can get him to agree, I'll call you to pick up the list of renters."

Rachel rode with Ivy back to the cemetery, while Sutton followed in his truck, keeping an eye out for any signs of outside surveillance. If there was anyone stalking him or Ivy, he didn't spot them during the drive, and they returned to the cemetery without incident.

Rachel's car was still parked just off the access road near Marjorie Kenner's new grave. Hers was the only car left when Ivy pulled up and parked behind the Honda Accord; all of the other mourners had left already.

Ivy got out with Rachel and exchanged a few words that Sutton couldn't hear. She waited outside the Jeep until Rachel was safely inside her car and driving away. But as she turned to get back into her Jeep, she stopped suddenly, her gaze directed toward the newly dug grave. Moving slowly at first, then gaining speed, she started walking up the modest incline toward the grave.

Sutton got out of the truck and followed, catching up at the grave. "What is it?"

Ivy crouched beside the grave and pulled a pair of latex gloves from her pocket. As he watched with confusion, she reached out and examined a small flowering green plant that seemed to have been planted at the head of the grave, close to where the small granite nameplate lay, a placeholder until the family could arrange for a proper grave marker.

"I saw this same plant at Coral Vines's grave," she told Sutton, pushing to her feet. She started walking across the graveyard, leaving him to keep up, and stopped a few plots away at a second grave. "See?"

He bent to examine the plant growing next to the simple gravestone. "I think I know what this is," he told her, feeling a strange quiver in the middle of his gut. "It's belladonna."

"That's—"

"Deadly nightshade," he finished for her.

"I don't see any of those plants on the other graves around here."

"Could be a coincidence," he suggested, not sounding convincing even to his own ears.

She started walking again, moving at a determined clip. He caught up and followed her to a third grave. The headstone read "Amelia Sanderson."

With her foot, Ivy nudged a leafy plant growing by the grave, making the leaves and star-shaped purple flowers gently shake. The flowers alternated with darkening purple berries—belladonna again, Sutton recognized. "Same plant, right?" Ivy asked.

He nodded. "The whole plant is poisonous."

She scanned the graveyard, then started walking again. By the time they stopped at a fourth grave, Sutton wasn't surprised to find a fourth belladonna plant growing near the headstone of April Billings's grave.

"It's his calling card," he said.

Ivy looked up at him. "What does that do to the idea that these murders are professional hits?"

He rubbed his jaw. "I don't know."

"Could these plants have gotten here by natural means? Birds scattering seeds or something like that?" Ivy asked.

"I don't think so—it's not a native plant in this area."

She bent and grabbed leaves, flowers and berries from the plant, stripping off her latex glove inside out and tying the end to create a makeshift evidence bag. Pulling more gloves from her pocket, she repeated the process at each of the other three grave sites until she had samples from each. "I'll get these tested to be sure we're right about what they are."

He nodded. "Good idea."

"Meanwhile, I'm going to go talk to our surveillance teams. We've had the cemetery under surveillance since the third murder."

In case the killer wanted to spend some quality time with his kills, Sutton thought with approval. It made sense. "Nobody's reported anything unusual?"

"No." Her dark eyebrows flicked upward. "But maybe I haven't been asking the right questions."

IT WAS LATE IN THE afternoon before Ivy heard back from the Knoxville botanist with whom she'd left the plant cuttings. While waiting for word, she'd spent most of her time sifting through the stacks of surveillance notes and photos from the shifts of two-man teams who'd kept the cemetery under watch for the past three weeks.

Nothing jumped out at her as significant in the surveillance files. Photos showed exactly what she'd have expected to see at a graveyard—mourners, grounds crews, regular weekly visitors to specific graves. She saw nothing that struck her as significant.

The call from Dr. Phelps at the University of Tennessee proved more interesting. "It's definitely *Atropa belladonna*," Dr. Phelps told her. "Deadly nightshade, in the vernacular."

"And it's not a native species here in eastern Tennessee?"

"It's not a native plant, but it's a cultivated plant species here in the States, so it's not that strange to find it growing. It has weedlike characteristics such as self-cultivation."

"So it could have gotten into the cemetery naturally?"

"Theoretically," Dr. Phelps agreed. "But from your description of where you found the plants, I'd say they were deliberately planted there. The sheer odds against the plants all self-cultivating in the same general area of the grave, near the headstone? It just defies belief."

"Is there any way to trace where the plant originated?"

"Possibly. But any tests we could run would, at the very least, require that you find the original rootstock."

"Are there legitimate reasons to cultivate the plant?"

"Oh, absolutely. Atropine, which derives from *Atropa belladonna,* is an anticholinergic agent. It's a common treatment for organophosphate poisoning."

"It's a poison but it's also a poison antidote?" Ivy asked, confused.

"Not an antidote per se. In the right dosage, it blocks acetylcholine—" Dr. Phelps cut off the explanation, as if he sensed he was only making things less clear for Ivy.

"Basically, it limits the effectiveness of poisons attacking the nervous system. Soldiers in battle who might encounter chemical weapons generally carry atropine injectors with them as an antidote."

"Do you know of any growers here in Tennessee who cultivate belladonna?"

"Not off the top of my head. I could look into it for you."

"That would be great. Thank you."

"You've got a lead?" Antoine Parsons had come into the bull pen while she was talking to Dr. Phelps. He'd perched on her desk until she'd finished the call.

"I'm not sure I'd call it a lead exactly. It's more like a whole new set of questions." She caught him up on the plants she'd found in the cemetery. "What about you? Anything new?" Antoine had gone out to recanvass the neighborhoods around the previous victims' homes, with the potential truck angle in mind.

"People apparently don't pay that much attention to trucks driving through their neighborhoods," Antoine answered with a grimace. "They're not uncommon sights, and unless the damned thing's painted pink with yellow polka dots or something, a truck driving through the neighborhood barely pings the radar."

She'd known it was a long shot. "It was worth a try."

"How about Davenport Trucking? Anything from them yet?"

She shook her head. "I'm trying not to be impatient. Her father seemed really adamant about protecting his clients' privacy. I don't blame him. They do have a certain expectation that their private information stays that way."

"But one of those people could be a serial killer."

Or a hit man, she added silently, thinking about what Sutton had shared with her the night before.

The call she'd been hoping for came around three that

afternoon. Rachel Davenport's voice, harried and soft, greeted her with, "I talked my father into giving you the rental records."

"Rachel, thank you so much!" She waved at Antoine, covering the receiver. "We're getting the rental records."

"He only agreed to give you the records from the past month and a half," Rachel added, "but if you think the killer chose his victims during that time period, that should be enough, shouldn't it?"

Ivy hoped so. "When can I pick them up?"

"I'm going to pull the records tonight after work. I can get them to you either later tonight or in the morning."

"I can come by the place tonight to pick them up," Ivy offered, eager to get to work on the list. She wouldn't be able to call or question any of the people on the rental roster until morning, but maybe the list itself would supply a vital clue to the identity of the killer.

"I may not get it done until late."

"That's okay. I can come by and give you company so you won't have to be alone there so late."

"That would be nice." There was a faintly wistful tone to Rachel's voice, a reminder that the woman had just lost four people close to her in the past month and a half. Her mother had died when Rachel was young, and now her father was dying of cancer.

Ivy wasn't sure how the woman was even standing upright these days.

She ran home after work to change into more casual clothes and grab a bite to eat before she headed over to Maryville. To her surprise, she found Sutton Calhoun sitting on her front porch steps again. No beer this time, but the look in his eyes was just as dangerous as it had been the day before.

"You done playing cop for the day?" He rose to his

feet when she got out of the Jeep and started walking toward him.

"Playing cop?" She arched her eyebrows at his choice of words.

"Being. Excelling at. Whatever." He walked toward her, meeting her halfway. He smelled clean and crisp, as if he'd grabbed a shower after the funeral. He looked good, too, clean-shaven and clear-eyed.

She'd thought her vulnerability to him the day before had been greatly magnified by his emotional turmoil. After all, she'd always been a sucker for a sob story, a weakness she'd had to fight on the job.

But a confident, strong-willed Sutton Calhoun seemed to have no trouble appealing to her libido, either. Which meant she had no immunity to Sutton at all. He appealed to her no matter what he had going on in his life.

"I'm hungry," he said with a slow, simmering smile. "You hungry?"

"I could eat," she answered, trying hard not to make her response sound like an innuendo. The slow burn in Sutton's hazel eyes suggested she hadn't succeeded. Nor did she do herself any favors by adding, "What do you have in mind?"

His lips curved. "Something hot. Tasty."

He wasn't even pretending to be coy anymore. "You're in an interesting mood this afternoon."

He'd moved close enough that the slightest move forward would put her in contact with him. "Interesting in a good way?" he asked.

She felt as if her whole body was straining toward him, and it took all the willpower she had not to give in. There was too much at stake to jump back into anything with Sutton Calhoun. Too damned much to lose.

"Do you really want to get dinner somewhere? Or do you just want to drive me crazy?"

He lifted his hand, sliding his finger along the curve of her collarbone where it lay exposed in the scoop neckline of her blouse. "Am I driving you crazy?"

"Wasn't that your intention?" She tried to keep her answer cool and composed, but it was nearly impossible to maintain her cool when Sutton was tracing fire across her skin with his touch.

"I like the way your skin flushes when I touch you." His voice was little more than a whisper. "It lets me know I'm not the only one feeling things between us."

"Sutton, what are we doing here?" She tried to walk away from his touch, but her legs refused to cooperate.

His brows notched upward. "Flirting, I thought."

"But what do you want from me?" So much for keeping her cool. Desperation painted every word that spilled from her lips.

He laughed. "You want me to describe it in detail?"

She did. She wanted him to paint word pictures of everything he wanted to do to her and wanted her to do to him. Then she wanted to go inside her house and play out the images in her head for real, leaving out nothing, not a touch, not a taste, not a stroke.

But giving up that last vestige of control to Sutton would be a grave mistake. She'd given him her heart years ago. Her soul was probably his, too. All she had left that belonged to her was her body, and if she gave Sutton control over that part of her as well, she wasn't sure she'd survive it this time when he left.

And he would leave. He had leaving etched on every inch of his body. Sooner or later, he'd dust off the Tennessee clay and head back to wherever he called home today.

And she'd be all alone here in Bitterwood, just as before, with twice as many grievous wounds.

She made herself step out of his reach. "I have plans tonight."

"Dinner plans?" His eyes narrowed slightly, as if it occurred to him for the first time that she might have a romantic life of her own. She supposed she could pretend she had a date. Save a little face, at least.

But she'd never been much good at game playing. "Rachel Davenport is putting together the truck rental files for us after work this evening. I told her I'd come pick them up."

"So we'll grab something to eat on the way," Sutton said. "Call and see if she wants us to get something for her. We'll feed her for her trouble."

Damn it, she thought. Just when she thought she had it in her to resist his charms, he went and came up with a thoughtful idea that she hadn't even considered. "I'll call her and ask if I can bring her something. No need for you to bother."

"I'm hungry, you're hungry—"

"What do you want from me?" she snapped, regretting the words instantly. His expression went from an easy smile to uneasy wariness. "I'm sorry. That was a stupid, uncalled-for question."

"Right now," he said carefully, "I just want dinner with someone whose company I enjoy. Can we just go with that?"

She felt like an idiot, especially since he was being so reasonable. "We can go with that." Nice and casual.

Except she didn't think she could ever be just casual where Sutton Calhoun was concerned.

Chapter Eleven

Davenport Trucking looked deserted when Sutton drove into the lot and parked in front of the main office. "Are you sure she's here?" he asked Ivy, who was balancing their bags of takeout on her knees in the passenger seat.

"She said she'd be in the back office and to ring the bell." Ivy carefully shifted the bags as she reached for the door handle. One of the sweet teas started to tip over in its carrying tray, and Sutton snaked out a hand to snare it before it spilled, stretching close enough to Ivy that he could smell the lingering aroma of apple-scented shampoo in her dark hair.

She turned to look at him, her pupils wide. He knew the signs of arousal, saw the flush in her cheeks, the way her lips trembled apart and the pulse in her throat began to race. He felt his own body's quickening response and considered how easy it would be to let nature take its course.

But would it be wise? Sexual attraction was one of those things that the mind couldn't always control, and the object of desire could sometimes come as a disconcerting surprise.

"What are you thinking?" Ivy asked, her dark eyes narrowing slightly.

"How much I want to kiss you," he answered before he

could stop himself. The flush in her cheeks spread to the hint of skin he could see in the V of her cotton sweater.

"Sutton—"

He sat back, turning to face the windshield. Frustration sang in his blood but he willed himself to stay controlled. "What are we doing here? Is that what you were going to ask?"

"I guess you find my caution tedious," she said in a prim tone that made him want to laugh. But laughter had hurt her feelings before, and the one thing he knew beyond a doubt was that he didn't want to hurt Ivy Hawkins.

"I don't find anything about you tedious," he said truthfully. "There's not a second I spend in your company that I regret."

"You do have your daddy's talent for pretty talk," she said with a lopsided smile that made his chest ache.

"I'm just telling you the truth."

"Then admit my caution frustrates you."

He slanted a helpless look at her. "Yeah. It definitely frustrates me."

"I guess a guy like you doesn't get stop signs very often."

"Often enough," he assured her with a wry smile.

"I'm just not good at this—this whatever it is that's going on between us," she said. "I don't know how to be smart or sophisticated about it."

"I guess it's my turn to ask a question," he said, suddenly curious to hear her answer. "What do *you* want to get out of whatever this is that we have between us?"

She gazed back at him as if the question had confused her. "I've learned not to have expectations about relationships."

Because of her mother, he realized. Even back when he was a boy, Arlene Hendry had been known as a serial sweetheart, one of the kinder terms used to describe her. She'd never married Ivy's father, though she'd given Ivy his last name, despite his refusal to acknowledge his paternity. She'd gone from one man to the next, ever the starry-eyed romantic certain that this one would be Mr. Right. It was one of the reasons Ivy had turned to him for friendship and understanding—they'd both known what it was like to have to live down their families' reputations.

"You have a right to expectations," he said in a gentle tone.

Her expression fell. "Don't pity me."

"I don't pity you any more than I pity myself." He shook his head. "Neither of our parents did us any favors."

"How am I supposed to trust myself to make good decisions? Where would I have learned such a lesson? I've watched my mother fall in love dozens of times, with all the staying power of a piece of cheap gum." She tightened her grip on one of the food bags as it started to slip, her knuckles turning white. "She gets hurt every single time, but she just keeps on. I don't want to be that woman. I don't want to get hurt over and over again and keep going back for more."

"The last thing I want to do is hurt you."

"But you will. Everyone hurts everyone else. That's just part of the game." She nudged the tray of drinks toward him. "Here, take these."

He took them from her lap. She slid out of the front seat and landed lightly next to the truck, still holding on to the bags. He hurried around to catch up with her as she walked up the sidewalk to the office front door.

"I don't think it has to be part of the game," Sutton said as she pushed the doorbell. "I don't think relationships have to be a game."

She looked up at him, her expression thoughtful in the harsh glow of the parking lot lights. "Don't you?"

Movement from inside the office gave him an excuse not to answer, a good thing, since he wasn't sure he knew how to argue a concept he'd never believed himself. Love, in his experience, created more problems than it solved. It weakened the soul, addled the brain and generally caused nothing but grief for everyone involved.

At least, he'd always thought that until he'd started working for Cooper Security. The Coopers had somehow found a way to combine satisfying, challenging work and happy marriages without the world ending. Maybe it helped that they and their spouses worked in the same general field. Maybe it was just blind luck, although what were the odds that a whole family would be so lucky? Sutton didn't know the answer.

He just knew he had never seen himself as a good candidate for happily ever after, even if he'd recently begun to wonder what he might be missing.

"I'm about halfway through the list," Rachel said as greeting as she opened the door. She looked tired, Sutton thought. She wasn't wearing any makeup that might hide the purple shadows under her reddened eyes. Her connection to all four of the murder victims had to have taken a toll on her emotions.

"We brought food." He pulled one of the teas from the carrier. "Hope you like sweet tea."

She looked at the cup of tea. "Thank you. I forgot to eat lunch, and here I was about to skip dinner, as well."

"That's not good for you. I know you've had a lot to handle, between losing your friends and your father's illness, but you have to make time to take care of yourself," Ivy said, her voice tinted by real concern. "Barbecue and chips aren't the most nutritional things we could have given you, but at least it's fuel, right?"

"Thank you." Rachel managed a faint smile as she took the cup from Sutton. "I hate to be antisocial, but if I'm going to finish working out the list for you tonight, I need to be without distractions, so…"

"So be quiet and don't bother you?" Ivy finished with a laugh.

Rachel made a regretful face. "Well, I wouldn't have said it that way, but…"

Sutton handed her a wrapped barbecue sandwich and a bag of potato chips. "How quiet should we be?"

"You don't have to be quiet." Rachel managed a real smile. "I'll be playing music—it helps me concentrate. So don't feel as if you need to whisper."

"Are there that many rented trucks that qualify for your list?" Ivy asked, her brow furrowed. She was probably thinking about how much legwork she and Antoine would have to do to mark all the names off that list, Sutton thought. He didn't envy her the grunt work, but he sure would like to get his hands on that list.

He wouldn't, unfortunately. Ivy had been clear with him about that point on the drive to Maryville. "She's allowing this without a warrant because she trusts me to be discreet. I'm not going to ask her to include you in that mix. You're just going to have to trust that I'll do my job."

He did trust her, he realized, despite having seen her in action such a short time. She was smart, she was driven and she was stubborn, all good qualities in a detective. She wanted the case solved, with far less financial incentive than Sutton himself had to close the case.

"More than I realized," Rachel answered Ivy's question. "I'm having to include some trucks that are on a long-term rental contract, since you're looking for all Davenport trucks that could be on the road during the time period, right? Not just trucks rented during that period."

"Right," Ivy agreed quickly. "We'll stay out here and let you work."

"You can use the conference room table to eat—first door on the right."

As Rachel went into the back office and closed the door behind her, Sutton nodded toward the door Rachel had indicated. "Shall we?"

They settled at one end of a long, well-polished oak table in an otherwise spare, utilitarian conference room, Ivy at the head of the table and Sutton taking the chair at her right. Ivy slanted a look at him. "You must be wondering why I called this meeting," she intoned.

He groaned at the old joke.

Ivy laughed, opening the bag of food. "I have a feeling I'd better eat up. If that list of names is as long as I think it's going to be, Antoine and I will be hoofing it for days, trying to talk to everyone and account for their whereabouts during the murders. Or, I guess, we're really going to be accounting for the whereabouts of the trucks they've rented, since it's possible someone other than the renters could have access to the vehicles." Her brow wrinkled. "Goody."

"If you asked, Rachel Davenport would probably agree to let me help you and Antoine out with the legwork."

She stopped in the middle of unwrapping a sandwich. "You're right. She'd probably agree, and sure, Antoine and I could use the help beating the bushes. But if Rayburn even knew you were sitting here with me while I waited for this list, he'd take me off the case. And I don't want off this case."

He felt like a jerk for pressuring her now. She'd been more accommodating than he'd have been in her position. "You're right. I should be following my own leads."

"Except your leads are my leads," she said in a resigned tone. Lowering her voice, she added, "I'm not alone in thinking it's strange that all four of the victims were connected to Rachel Davenport in some way, am I?"

"No, you're not." He'd been thinking about the coincidence ever since they'd discovered that Rachel had considered Marjorie Kenner a close friend. "That poor woman—she's lost four friends in the last month or so, and her father is dying of liver cancer. No wonder she looks beaten down and tired."

"If we hadn't brought her food, I wonder if she'd have bothered to eat."

"You remember how I told you about Seth Hammond getting approached to do a contract killing?"

"I do. Which reminds me, I need to have a long talk with him about keeping that kind of information to himself." Ivy's lips flattened with annoyance for a moment, then her brow furrowed. "Oh. I get where you're going. It's all about the victim. And all the victims were close to Rachel Davenport."

Sutton nodded. "What if these killings are really all about one victim? Rachel Davenport."

"But why? Does that poor woman in there really seem like someone who'd inspire that level of malice? She doesn't even look capable of hurting a fly, much less drawing enough wrath to warrant a contract killing."

"But they're not trying to kill her. The contract isn't out on her."

"Isn't it?" Ivy put down her half-eaten sandwich and leaned toward him, close enough that he got another whiff of warm, clean scent. "What if it really is targeting her in some way? Look at how hard she's taken these deaths. If you wanted to punish her, to make her suffer—"

"So this is some sort of twisted stalker thing? Hurting her by hiring someone to kill the people she cares about?" Sutton couldn't hide his skepticism. The idea sounded crazy.

"I don't know!" Ivy's voice rose with frustration. She lowered it, glancing toward the door. "I don't know. I just know that all of this has something to do with Rachel Davenport. Whether she's the trigger that's setting this killer off or she's the target of some sort of backhanded murder-for-hire scheme, I cannot shake the conviction that these murders are somehow about her."

Sutton wanted to argue with her. Contract murders were generally about getting an inconvenient person out of the way or punishing someone for a perceived wrong. They weren't about torturing a person with grief.

But contract murders also didn't play out like serial murders, with clear signatures and identical M.O.s. Yet he'd been seriously considering the idea that the four Bitterwood murders may have been committed by someone hired to do so.

Make it look like anything but a hit....

"Maybe we should just table all the crazy theorizing until I get my hands on that list and see where it takes me," Ivy said, picking up her sandwich again.

They fell quiet while they ate, strains of music from the office down the hall filling the silence. Rachel Davenport's taste ran to classic rock, apparently, and the evening DJ on the classic rock station was playing a commercial-free set of Southern rock ballads. Lynyrd Skynyrd's "Free Bird" was the current choice, evoking memories of lazy summer nights parked at Summerford Overlook, listening to the classic rock station out of Knoxville and trying to get past second base with whatever pretty little mountain girl he'd been seeing at the time.

"Makes me wish I had a lighter to wave," he murmured, winning a grin from Ivy.

"My mother has all kinds of stories about seeing Skynyrd in concert." Ivy finished off her sandwich and rolled the wrapper into a neat ball. Her smile faded. "I'm fairly sure she met at least one of my many 'uncles' at a concert."

"I just remember envying you for even having a mother," Sutton admitted. "Maybe she made bad decisions and screwed up her life, but she was there for you when you fell down and skinned your knees. Remember?"

Ivy's expression softened. "She was. She tried to give me a family, really. That's what all those men were about. Not just her wanting to feel loved but also wanting me to have something my own daddy didn't stick around to give me. I know all that."

"Still, it's hard to forget the bad stuff." He thought about his father, stuck there in his house, in a body that wouldn't work right anymore and a voice, once his most powerful resource, that couldn't weave a story any longer. He felt sorry for him, but he couldn't forgive him. Not yet. Maybe not ever.

He tore his mind away from the unpleasant past and rose to his feet, holding out his hand to Ivy as an Eagles song replaced Lynyrd Skynyrd on the radio. "Take It to the Limit"—one of his favorites.

Ivy eyed his outstretched hand, her expression wary.

"Come on, Hawkins. Everybody can handle a slow dance. Even a clumsy little mountain girl like you."

Her eyes narrowed with mock outrage. "Oh, now you've asked for it." She took his hand and let him pull her to her feet, moving willingly into the circle of his arms. She lifted her chin, her dark eyes flashing a challenge he wanted more than anything to meet.

She had a natural feel for the music, her body catching

the rhythm and making it part of her. And damn, she felt good in his arms. He wondered what would have happened if he'd stuck around all those years ago instead of leaving. When she was seventeen and he was twenty, would he have taken her to her high school prom?

Would they have been married with babies by the time they reached their thirties?

But he'd left. And those were questions that would never get answered now. Still, there were some questions she could answer for him, at least. Answers about the years of her life he'd missed because he'd left Bitterwood behind.

"Who took you to your prom?" he asked, bending closer to whisper in her ear, trying to remember some of the kids her age in town. "Tommy Adler, maybe? I know, Josh Belholland. He was always sniffing around you back in the day—"

"Who said I went to the prom?"

"The boys 'round here are idiots, then." She felt warm and soft pressed against him, moving in gentle sways to the music. He felt his hand creeping downward, toward her backside, and almost let it reach its goal before stopping right at the curve of her waist. She was in his arms, one hand moving in light, shiver-inducing circles across his lower back. He'd be an idiot himself to do anything to change that situation.

"Maybe if you'd stuck around Bitterwood, you could've asked me." She said it lightly, as if making a joke, but there was a serious undertone to her voice.

"I was just thinking about that myself," he said, infusing his words with a smile. "I'd have been a little old for you at the time, maybe, but as we got older, it wouldn't have mattered."

She shook her head. "I'm not sure you'd have looked

at me any differently when I was seventeen and you were twenty. Our relationship was never like that."

"By that time, your mama pretty much hated the name 'Calhoun,' didn't she? Remember how you had to sneak around to see me toward the end?"

"I remember." She laid her head against his shoulder. He breathed in the scent lingering in her hair. "I still haven't told her you're back in town."

"Afraid she'd forbid you from seeing me?"

Ivy looked up, flashing him a look full of amused consternation. "If she was smart."

He brushed his lips against her temple as he pulled her closer. "Then I'm glad she doesn't know."

They danced quietly through another ballad, this one a plaintive plea for forgiveness from .38 Special. "I think I'd have wanted you back then," Sutton whispered in her ear. "Lord knows I want you now."

Her breath came out in a shaky little hiss as she lifted her head to meet his gaze. "Sutton."

He bent his head slowly, giving her time to change her mind. But she rose to her toes, her lips parting as she curled her fingers around his neck.

Lights flashed suddenly through the conference room window from outside, painting the wall with bright streaks. Sutton turned in time to see a truck moving past the front of the building out of sight.

"We can't be this lucky," Ivy murmured, already moving out of his arms.

Sutton followed her out of the conference room and through the front door, his hand settling on the butt of his Glock where it nestled in a waistband holster behind his back. Ivy had drawn her weapon, moving fast but with stealth, angling her approach from the side of the building to maintain cover as long as possible.

A truck had come to a stop at the self-serve cleaning station, the back doors angled just in front of the drain.

While they'd been inside the building, the last of twilight had faded into inky darkness, punctuated by circles of muddy yellow light cast by the tall lamps that flanked the parking lot. Close to the building, however, darkness reigned, rendered even blacker when compared with those oases of light.

Ahead, Ivy was little more than a compact silhouette creeping through the gloom. She'd changed out of her work suit into a pair of dark jeans and a black cotton sweater that hugged her curves in all the right places but served as a successful bit of camouflage in the night. From behind, he could see only the pale flesh of her hands and the occasional flash of skin beneath the wavy mass of her ponytail.

From the angle where they were, the corner of the office building nearly hid the cleaning bay from view. Only the back end of the truck remained visible as they moved closer. So far, nobody had gotten out to open the truck and commence with the washing.

Ivy slowed to a stop at the corner and Sutton slipped into place behind her. One hand reached out behind her, as if to reassure herself he was there. He touched her fingers, and she squeezed hers around his for a moment, before drawing away to sneak a peek around the corner.

She ducked back quickly, flattening herself against the building as a man came into view. He was tall and lean, in his early forties and dressed in dirty gray coveralls spotted with what looked, in the artificial light, like splashes of ink.

"Let him show us what's inside," Ivy whispered, her voice little more than a breath against his cheek.

The man unlocked the back door of the truck, stepping back quickly as he swung it open. Thick, dark red liquid began to trickle out immediately, aided by gravity from the truck's slightly inclined position.

Sutton's gut tightened. Even from the distance of several feet, the sickly metallic odor was unmistakable.

Blood.

Chapter Twelve

For a moment, Sutton thought Ivy was going to slingshot out from the shelter of the building and take down the man by herself. But even as her muscles bunched to strike, she swung around suddenly toward him, her eyes glimmering in the low light.

"No jurisdiction," she breathed, even that tiny bit of sound thick with frustration.

He hadn't even thought of jurisdiction, he realized. He'd been too focused on getting a better look at what the man was up to.

"I don't need jurisdiction," he whispered in her ear, his lips brushing the delicate curve of cartilage.

She clutched the front of his shirt. "Sutton—"

He pressed a swift kiss on her forehead and moved out into the open, keeping his hand on the Glock. He walked quietly, his gaze on the man who now stood with his back to the building, watching the blood drip out of the inclined truck.

"May I help you?" Sutton asked.

The man jumped at the sound of Sutton's voice, and he whirled to face him. "Who are you?"

"Security," Sutton answered. It wasn't a complete lie.

"Oh." The man relaxed. "Look, I know this is after hours, but I've done this before and nobody ever complained, so I didn't think—" He stopped rambling and took a deep breath. "The butcher was late getting to my hogs, which meant I was late getting them to the meat market. I couldn't wait till morning, see? I don't have cold storage anywhere big enough."

Sutton listened to the man's explanation, studying his body language with a practiced eye. He seemed relaxed enough, if a little flustered. "What's your name?"

"David Pennock. My brothers and I run Pennock Farm over in Walland."

"Nice place." Ivy came into the open, her weapon holstered and her hands by her sides. "I went to college in Chattanooga with your brother a few years back."

Pennock's smile looked friendly. "Must've been Kevin. Only one of us with a damn bit of brains."

"You've done this before?" Sutton asked.

"You mean clean out the truck after hours?" Pennock nodded. "Not real often, but sometimes if things get backed up at Merchant Brothers—that's the butcher we use—we get behind delivering the fresh cuts of meat to the area markets that carry our products."

"Aren't there sanitation rules about carrying raw meat?" Ivy asked, moving around the truck to look at the open doors at the back. Sutton crossed to her side and looked into the truck.

There were large electric coolers built into the inner walls of the truck, he saw. "If you carry the meat products in there, why is there all this blood in the truck?"

"One of our pallets broke when we were loading a couple of dressed whole hogs—we have a couple of customers who prefer to do the processing themselves, so we let Merchant Brothers slaughter the hogs and drain their blood. Apparently one big old fellow had an aneurysm somewhere in his system that didn't bust until we dropped him on the way into the truck. Made an unholy mess, but since all the other meat is kept in the coolers, which are sanitized daily, I figured we could wait until after delivery to clean out the mess in the truck." Pennock looked defensive. "Other people do it, too. I mean, nobody ever said there was a rule about it."

"Other people?" Ivy asked. "You've seen other trucks being cleaned out after hours?"

Pennock's brow furrowed. "You're security, too?"

"Actually, she's a police officer." Sutton didn't mention the different jurisdiction.

"Oh. This is against the law or something?" Pennock looked alarmed. "I swear I didn't know. I won't ever do it again."

"Did you see other trucks cleaned out after hours?" she repeated, ignoring his sudden nervousness.

Pennock glanced at Sutton, as if looking for moral support. "A time or two."

"Recently?"

"I saw one maybe a month ago," Pennock answered. "Is there something going on?"

"Do you remember anything about the truck you saw a month ago?" Ivy pressed.

He shook his head. "It was just a truck. They were parked here and some guy was mucking out the back. That's how I got the idea it was okay to clean up after hours."

"Do you remember what was in the back?"

Pennock's alarm was back. "No. Just something wet. I didn't get a good look. I don't even remember if there was any sort of sign on the side."

Ivy looked at Sutton, frustration lining her features. As she opened her mouth to say something, Sutton's phone buzzed in his pocket. He gave her an apologetic look and moved away from them, checking the number. It was a local Tennessee area code, the number unfamiliar. Sutton almost ignored the call. But at the last moment before it went to voice mail, he answered. "Sutton Calhoun."

"Sutton, it's Seth. Your daddy's had a fall and he's in the E.R."

"It's a clean break of the humerus, about three inches above the elbow." Cleve Calhoun's doctor was a very young orthopedic surgeon who had introduced himself as Dr. Choudry. What he lacked in age and experience, he made up for in composure and confidence. "Right now he's stable and resting under a mild sedative. We were able to realign the bones without surgery, but given his age and his stroke-related disabilities, we'll want to keep him in the hospital for at least three more days, until we're satisfied he can deal with the cast and its limitations on his movement."

Sutton wanted to feel relieved that his father's injury wasn't far worse. It certainly could have been—Seth had looked pale and pinched when he greeted Sutton's arrival to the River Bend Medical Center, as if the past few hours had taken years off his life span. "He tried walking on his own," Seth had explained on the elevator ride to the fourth-floor waiting room.

"Why would he do such a thing?"

Seth had looked reluctant to answer.

"What aren't you telling me?" Sutton had pushed.

"He kept yelling your name as he got up," Seth had replied. "I heard him all the way from the kitchen, but by the time I got there, he'd already taken a tumble." Seth had led him down the hall to the waiting area, where several other people sat in groups of two or three around the large room, but it wasn't so crowded that they'd had trouble finding a couple of seats to themselves away from the others.

"You heard him say my name?"

"One of the clearest things I've heard him say," Seth had admitted.

"What do you think it means?" The question had spilled from his lips before he could stop it.

"Maybe seeing you reminded him of what he used to be like," Seth had suggested. "Could be he wants to be like that again."

They'd waited another half hour before Dr. Choudry had arrived to catch them up on his father's condition.

"Do you have any questions?" Dr. Choudry asked.

It was Seth, not Sutton, who answered. "His head was bleeding like it had cracked open. You didn't even mention that."

"It was a superficial cut. Head wounds can often bleed profusely. But the EMTs said he hadn't lost consciousness, and the CAT scan showed no signs of a closed head injury. We'll keep an eye on his vitals, but I don't see any reason for concern. You're free to visit with him until visiting hours are over. Just be aware that the medication we gave him to ease the pain of his break will make him drowsy, so he may not be in a sociable mood."

After the doctor left, Seth started toward the door immediately, but all Sutton could do was drop into the nearest seat, leaning forward, his head resting on his hands.

"You're not going with me to visit him?" Seth sounded incredulous.

Sutton looked up at the other man. "There's a lot of bad blood between Cleve and me. You know that."

"He's a sick old man who could use a little human kindness." Seth's expression shifted to a smile as false as the anxiety in his green eyes was real. "Lord knows, he won't get much human kindness from an old scammer like me, right?"

"He always liked you."

Seth shrugged. "Kindred souls."

"You've taken care of him."

"So?" Seth's tone was defensive.

"So, thanks."

Sutton could tell that Seth didn't know how to respond to gratitude. He probably hadn't gotten many kind words of any sort in a long time. Not that Sutton could feel very sorry for him. Seth Hammond had made his choices with his eyes wide open. He'd hurt his share of innocent people over the years, following in Cleve's duplicitous footsteps. He'd earned his bad reputation fair and square.

"I think he'd like to see you," Seth said a moment later, filling the uncomfortable silence.

"I think he'd like to see you more."

"It's not a competition."

Maybe it wasn't. But if his father had risked his neck trying to prove his manhood just because Sutton had bothered to come around after fourteen years of silence, the old man probably wouldn't appreciate Sutton bearing witness to his failure.

"You can tell him I'm here. If he wants to see me, I'll go."

Seth studied him through narrowed eyes. "Okay. You're right. That's the way to handle it."

Sutton waited until Seth left the waiting room to pull out his cell phone and check his messages. He had a routine check-in call from the office. He handled that with a quick text to Jesse Cooper, reassuring him that everything was okay. The only other message was a text from Ivy.

Got the list and headed home. How's your dad?

He smiled at the brief message. A woman of few words, his Ivy.

He sent back a message reassuring her that his father

was doing well, considering, then sent a second message asking her to let him know if she found anything interesting in the list Rachel Davenport had given her.

He settled into his chair for a long wait, acutely aware of just how much he wished Ivy were there to keep him company.

The blood dripped slowly from the back of the truck, looking like crude oil in the glow of the high-pressure sodium vapor lamps that punctured the darkness in the parking lot with circles of yellow light. He breathed deeply, filling his lungs with the sweet metallic tang.

A flicker of movement from inside the building drew his attention away from his task. He didn't stare directly at the window where the woman stood, little more than a silhouette hovering at the edge of the frame. Instead, he framed her in his peripheral vision and went back to his cleaning.

He wished he had his rifle. It amplified his natural power, the weapon with its deadly load an appendage entirely under his control. Knives were toys. Exciting and stimulating. But like toys, their uses were largely limited to recreation. Yes, they could kill as well as entertain, but they were grossly inefficient as tools.

Rifles were coldly effective death-bringers. Utilitarian. Unsexy. But brutally efficient.

With a single shot, he could drill the life from the woman hovering at the window, watching him with a blend of curiosity and fear.

But this was the wrong situation for the rifle. He was too out in the open. Someone would hear and see.

The shadow in the building moved again. The knife in his pocket, wiped clean of all but the most microscopic of blood transfer, felt heavy and alive. How easily, he won-

*dered, could he subdue her and put her in the back of the
truck without drawing attention?*

So easily...

Ivy woke without transition, one second asleep and the
next awake. But the dream lingered, along with the metallic smell of blood. She knew it was just an olfactory
memory of the pig blood that had spilled from David Pennock's rented truck. Before she'd let Pennock leave, she'd
collected a blood sample on a clean square of gauze she'd
taken from Davenport Trucking's on-site first-aid kit. It
was currently air-drying in preparation for her taking it
to the Bitterwood Police Department's small crime scene
unit, which had kits that could rule out the possibility that
the blood she'd collected was human blood.

She was pretty sure Pennock had been telling the truth.
Rachel Davenport had positively identified him as one of
the company's longtime clients, and with a few calls she
had confirmed most of the rest of Pennock's story. The
blood test would simply provide a little reassurance that
her instincts were on target.

She'd fallen asleep at her desk again, her face pressed
into the list of names and businesses Rachel Davenport
had supplied. A quick check of her watch explained the
ache in her back; it was four-thirty in the morning. She'd
been asleep hunched over the desk for most of the night,
ever since Rachel had taken pity on her and delivered her
home to Bitterwood after Sutton—and her ride home—
had headed for the hospital in Knoxville.

She wondered if he was still there. She hadn't heard
from him other than a couple of brief text messages earlier that evening. Groaning, she rose from the desk chair
and stretched, promising herself that as soon as she closed
this case, she'd take a whole week off and do anything she

wanted. Which at this rate might be to sleep all day and all night.

Going back to sleep at this hour would only make her feel groggy all day, so she settled for a quick shower and two cups of strong, hot coffee to get her going. She took time to scramble a couple of eggs and toast slices of wheat bread for breakfast, settling at the kitchen table with the list of names she'd gotten from Davenport Trucking.

None of the names had caught her interest the first time through, and the second pass wasn't proving to be any more enlightening. She and Antoine would just have to go at the list the old-fashioned way—hoofing it from company to company to ask a few questions about where their rented trucks had been on the dates and times of the four murders.

She set the list aside and opened the file she'd compiled on the murders. The newest additions were color printouts of the images the surveillance crew covering the cemetery had sent her the day before. She'd already looked through them twice so far, but she flipped through the pages one more time, taking in the faces, many of them familiar, that had passed through the cemetery since she'd assigned the surveillance crew almost two weeks earlier.

Some of the faces she hadn't initially recognized were starting to become familiar now that she'd studied the photos for a while. There was a gray-haired woman who seemed to make daily visits to a grave located a few plots away from Amelia Sanderson's final resting place. Ivy jotted a note to herself to check who was buried there.

A teenage boy, tough-looking and rawboned, appeared in one of the photos. He caught Ivy's eye because his outer appearance seemed so at odds with the image he presented of a lost, terrified child as he stretched out on a plot of grass near Coral Vines's grave, his hand seeming to stroke the flat granite marker beneath his cheek.

She dragged her attention from that heartbreaking image and went to the next photo. In contrast, there was nothing particularly attention-catching about this photo, which looked like an outtake, a photo taken just to finish up a roll of film, though she knew it couldn't be anything like that, since the surveillance team used digital cameras.

It was a photo of people walking along the gravel-paved pathways between graves, none of them doing anything noteworthy. Unless you counted the buxom brunette near the center of the shot, she realized with a sudden flash of understanding. The dress she wore was thin and formfitting. It was also mostly see-through in the sunlight, and the photo had captured the full sheerness of the dress, revealing a low-cut demi-bra and tiny bikini panties beneath the flimsy fabric.

"Pigs," she muttered and started to move the photo aside. But something about the image snagged her attention. There were men in coveralls at work near the edge of the photo, planting what looked like pansies in small, round bucket planters that dotted the gravel walking paths at strategic intervals.

She backtracked through the previous images and found a few more shots of the landscapers at work. In one shot, the back of the coveralls was distinct enough that she could read the name of the company embroidered into the khaki fabric. Bramlett Nurseries.

Straightening, she grabbed the list of names she'd gotten from Davenport Trucking, running her finger down the column of renters until she found it. Bramlett Nurseries. Located right there in Bitterwood.

So Bramlett was the landscaper the cemetery used to maintain the grounds. And Bramlett rented a box truck from Davenport Trucking.

That had to mean something, didn't it?

She dug through the case file until she found a photo of

the belladonna plant she'd snapped at the cemetery after Marjorie Kenner's funeral. The plant was healthy and well-groomed, as if someone maintained it with care.

Someone like a horticulturist with his own nursery and landscaping company?

If workers from Bramlett Nurseries were tending to the plants at the grave sites, as they seemed to do in some of the surveillance pictures she'd quickly flipped through, would they recognize deadly nightshade for what it was?

IT WAS TOO EARLY TO GO to Bramlett Nurseries so she finished eating and dressed for work, heading in an hour and a half early to get a head start on the day. She had the detective's office to herself for only a few minutes, however, before Antoine Parsons wandered in with a doughnut, a cup of iced coffee and the morning paper. He looked surprised to see her there.

"Did you break the case?" he asked hopefully.

"Remains to be seen," she answered with a half smile. She waved him over and he pulled up a chair by her desk, listening with interest as she caught him up on what had happened since she'd left the office the day before. "It may mean nothing," she said after showing him the photos of the Bramlett Nurseries employees at work. "But it's at least an interesting coincidence that the nursery is a long-term renter from Davenport Trucking."

"That assumes you're right that the killer is using rented trucks as his killing field."

"Granted. But I think I am."

Antoine was quiet for a moment, his silent scrutiny making her feel like a germ under a microscope. Finally, he nodded. "I think you are, too."

"I've done a little preliminary checking this morning, made a few calls. Bramlett's been in business for years, although they were mostly a feed and seed shop until old Mr. Bramlett died last year. He didn't have any children, so the company went to his nephew Mark." She checked her notes. "I haven't been able to do much of a check on him, but the source who told me about old man Bramlett says the nephew lived in the Nashville area and moved here to take over the company."

"And changed up the way they did things, I take it?"

"Looks like. Modernized, added more decorative and landscaping plants for consumers, that sort of thing. The folks at Padgett Memorial said he's the one who pitched the groundskeeping job to them. They seem to think he's a nice guy."

"Nice guys can be killers," Antoine murmured.

Her cell phone rang. She checked the display. Sutton's name and number filled the small window. "Hawkins," she answered.

"Sorry I left you in a lurch. How'd you get home?"

"Rachel drove me," she answered casually, aware of Antoine's interest in the conversation. "How's your father?"

"Ornery, but the doctors seem sure he'll heal up quickly enough. It just can't be much fun to be in the hospital when you can't move around easily on your own." Sutton sounded nearly as frustrated as Ivy imagined his father must be feeling. "I slept in the waiting room. The sofas aren't as bad as they look."

"Really."

He made a soft huffing noise. "No, not really. They're as uncomfortable as sleeping on a pile of rocks. Is it okay if I go to your place and crash for a few hours?"

"Of course," she said. "I showed you where the key is."

"Thanks. You're a lifesaver. Any luck on the truck list yet?"

"Maybe." She didn't want to catch him up on all the details, not with Antoine listening in. She was already walking a razor-thin edge where Sutton and her investigation were concerned. "I'm going to spend the morning following up on a few things."

"You'll let me know what you learn?" There was a sexy undertone to his request, a reminder that his father had always been damned good at coaxing gullible women to fall in with his ideas and schemes—including her own mother once upon a time.

"I'll see you soon and we'll catch up." That was as much as she was willing to commit to. For all she knew, her visit to Bramlett Nurseries would prove to be a complete bust, and she'd have nothing to tell him at all.

Antoine was game when she suggested they head to Bramlett Nurseries first thing in order to be there when the place opened. "Catch them without any warning, and maybe we'll learn something useful."

Antoine drove while Ivy used her cell phone to look up Bramlett Nurseries on the internet. The company had a small, low-rent website, little more than a placeholder page with its address, phone number and hours of business. The nursery opened at eight, which meant they'd arrive right around the start of business.

The nursery was nestled in a pretty, tree-lined valley about five miles outside the Bitterwood city limits but still within the police department's jurisdiction. Behind the building, the Smoky Mountains slumbered like blue velvet giants, their softly rounded peaks shrouded by the pale morning mists that gave the mountain range its name.

The main building was boxy and rectangular, its utilitarian shape tempered by the quirky choice of colorful river stones as the primary building material. Behind the main building, three large greenhouses reflected the blue mountains and pearl-gray sky above them.

Inside the main building, Ivy and Antoine found a lone man behind the counter, his head down as he organized what looked like seed packets on the polished glass countertop. He didn't look up until he'd finished the task, his gray eyes calm and his expression neutral as he offered them a polite smile.

"Sorry for making you wait. But if I'd lost count, I'd have had to start over again." He swept the packets of seeds into a display box marked Bramlett Savoy Spinach and set them on the counter. "Can I help you?"

"I'd like to speak to whoever's in charge of your truck fleet."

The man at the counter smiled. "Fleet? We have a single truck for deliveries and landscaping jobs."

Ivy showed the man her shield. "I'm Detective Hawkins of the Bitterwood Police Department. This is Detective Parsons. Are you the manager?"

"Owner-operator," the man answered with a smile. "Mark Bramlett. Nice to meet you, Detectives. How can I help you?"

He did look like a nice guy, Ivy had to admit. Mid-thirties, sandy brown hair, tall and slim with friendly gray eyes. She'd probably buy a potted plant from him, she conceded, even though she had a notoriously brown thumb.

"Nice to meet you, too, Mr. Bramlett. We'd like to ask you some questions about the truck you rent from Davenport Trucking in Maryville."

Chapter Thirteen

"Did you get through to your pretty little cop?"

Sutton opened his eyes to find Seth Hammond sitting in the waiting room chair directly across from him. He looked tired and disheveled, but his green eyes were as sharp as ever. "I thought you were going home."

"I stopped in to check on Cleve and ended up staying until his pain pill kicked in and let him get back to sleep."

Once again, Sutton felt a twinge of guilt that it was Seth who was able to give his father comfort in his time of distress. All Sutton seemed to do when he visited his father was stress him out. "Is he any better at all?"

"He's resting a little easier." Seth shrugged. "Not sure if it's because he's actually in less pain or if he's just getting acclimated to it."

"He hates me, doesn't he?"

"I always figured it was the other way around."

"I don't hate him." At Seth's dubious look, Sutton added, "I just don't want to follow in his footsteps."

"He doesn't expect that. Hell, he doesn't even expect *me* to anymore."

"You've turned over a new leaf?" It was Sutton's turn to be skeptical.

Seth shrugged. "Call it what you want."

"Why?"

"Why'd I get out of the con game?" Seth rubbed his jaw, his palm making a swishing noise against his beard stubble. "I didn't like how people looked at me when they realized they'd been had. See, your daddy always treated it like a game. He's not actively trying to hurt people. He just wants to see what he can convince them to do to his benefit. He tried to teach me how to see it that way, but in the end, I couldn't. People got hurt, some real bad. Some might have deserved it for being greedy and stupid themselves, but a lot of them didn't. I just couldn't live with it."

"But you still watch out for Cleve."

"Somebody's got to."

"Are you trying to watch out for me, too?"

Seth's brow furrowed. "No idea what you're talking about."

"You left that marble on Ivy's porch for me to find. You knew I'd know who'd left it there. You knew I'd come looking for you."

"You ascribe a whole lot of knowledge to me—"

"You wanted to point me in the direction of Davenport Trucking, which suggests maybe you know more about these murders than you're letting on."

"First I'm the second coming of Ponzi and now I'm Ted Bundy?"

"I didn't say you committed them. But you know that Davenport Trucking is somehow involved. Did you know before you started working there or did you pick it up from being there day in and day out?"

"Rachel Davenport was close to all four of the murder victims. You've figured that out by now, haven't you?"

Sutton nodded.

"Ever wonder if that means something?"

He had, of course. He and Ivy had speculated about Rachel's connection to the cases just the night before. "What do you think it means?"

"I think George Davenport is dying, and there's a lucrative trucking company that's about to be looking for a new president. Right now, I'd reckon on Rachel Davenport being the obvious choice for the job. Which makes me wonder, why might someone be picking off Rachel Davenport's support system, one at a time?"

Sutton stared at Seth, a lot of loose puzzle pieces starting to click into place. "You think these really are murders for hire, don't you?"

Seth met his gaze with the intensity of a man who was sure he was right. "Don't *you?*"

He couldn't say no. The more he learned about the victims and the circumstances of the murders, the less they seemed to fit the pattern of a serial killer. The trappings were there, and Sutton had a feeling that the killer got some enjoyment out of the murders. But the only connection between the victims that made any sense at all was their connection to Rachel Davenport.

If she was the killer's focus, it would seem likely that she'd be a murder victim rather than a serial mourner. So whatever the motivation behind the murders, it wasn't about killing Rachel physically. It was about destroying her emotionally.

"Why would anyone want to hurt her that way?" he asked Seth. "Do you know anything about her?"

Seth was slow to answer. "A few things."

"Anything that would motivate someone to wreck her that way?"

"I'm not sure."

Sutton had the sense that Seth knew more than he was saying, but he didn't bother trying to press him directly. Seth could dig in his heels with the best of them. Instead, he changed topics. "Did you hang around here long after I left?"

"Yeah. I was in and out, but mostly in. Why?"

"I just get this sense—" He stopped, realizing whom he was talking to. When they'd been boys together up on Smoky Ridge, they'd shared everything, from tree forts to secret hiding caves. But then Seth Hammond had disappeared, sucked into the secrets and lies of Cleve's world. He wasn't Sutton's buddy. He wasn't his confidant. He sure as hell wasn't going to be Sutton's sounding board about Ivy Hawkins.

"You get what sense?"

"Nothing."

"You want to know what life was like for your daddy when you left?"

"No." He supposed he should feel guilty about that, but he just wasn't. Cleve had made the life he wanted, and he'd made it impossible for Sutton to stick around and be part of it without selling his soul.

"Ivy, then?" Seth's sharp green-eyed gaze met his directly. "You want to know what it was like for her when you hightailed it out of here?"

Sutton didn't answer. He supposed his silence was all the response Seth needed.

"For a little while, she just kept on going like always. I reckon part of her figured you'd come to your senses and come back here where you belonged. Then, when it became clear you weren't coming back, she started sticking around home with her mama a little more than usual. Turned out to be a big mistake, that."

The dark tone of Seth's voice made Sutton look up at his old friend. Seth looked angry.

Sutton's heart dropped. "What happened?"

"Billy Turlow happened." Seth's hands twisted around

each other as he spoke, the motions quick and almost violent. "Took up with her mama the summer after you left. Only it was clear to everybody but Arlene that the girl he really wanted was Ivy. I don't know all the details. The cops kept it pretty hushed up for a little town like this, but the basics got out. Seems one night, Ivy decided to take a kitchen knife to bed with her. Billy went into her bedroom, tried to force himself on her and took a knife in the side for his trouble."

"She killed him?"

"No, last I heard he was still alive. Nobody pressed any charges on anybody, but Billy Turlow left town as soon as he got out of the hospital, and Ivy went off to Chattanooga for a couple of years on a college scholarship. She didn't last there long. I guess her mama needed her too much."

Sutton felt sick. One of Ivy's deepest fears, he remembered, was that her mama was going to get raped or killed by one of the men she took home with her. Somehow, she'd never seemed to worry that she herself might be in danger.

But he'd worried. Not deeply, not daily, but from time to time, he'd noticed the way some of Arlene's fellows looked at her blossoming daughter and worried that they'd start wanting the young version more than her mother.

He'd figured it would cause more trouble between mother and daughter than create any sort of danger for Ivy herself. But he should have known better. He should have seen the signs of danger.

He'd just been too busy thinking about himself and planning his escape from Bitterwood and his father.

Mark Bramlett turned out to be friendly and accommodating, making Ivy wonder if the link between Bramlett Nurseries, Davenport Trucking and the nightshade found at the cemetery was nothing but a coincidence.

"We clean the truck out after every delivery or job," he told her as he let her take a look around inside the back of the rented panel truck while Antoine watched from a few feet away. "But we do the washing here at the nursery. I don't deal in products with special sanitation needs, so there's not much point in jumping through hoops to make sure the inside is sterile the way food processors do."

The interior of the truck looked freshly cleaned, she noted. "When was the last time you used it?"

"I had a crew out delivering seedlings to a retail outlet up in Knoxville just yesterday," he answered. "The crew washed it down when they got back."

"Would it be possible to speak to the employees who drive the truck?"

Bramlett shrugged. "Most of them are trained to handle trucks this size, so any one of them might be called on to drive it, depending on the job and the work crew on any given day. I do have a handful of workers who drive it more than others. I'll write up the list of names for you."

"Thank you," Ivy said with a grateful smile. "You've been very helpful."

"Glad to do it." Bramlett cocked his head, looking curious. "Is this anything to do with the murders in Bitterwood?"

"We're just following up on the possibility that one of these rental trucks could have been used in the commission of a crime."

"You think one of my employees used the truck to go out and kill those women?" Bramlett shook his head. "I know they say you can't always tell who's going to turn out to be a monster, but the guys we hire just don't seem the type."

"Most likely, your truck had nothing to do with any crime we might be investigating." Ivy kept her tone noncommittal. "We'll mark you off our list once we're done and that will be that."

"Just being thorough," Antoine added with a placid smile.

"Okay." Bramlett led them back inside and went behind the counter in search of paper and a pen. He jotted down a list of five names. "These guys do most of the driving, and they're responsible for making sure the truck is cleaned and locked before they leave at night."

Ivy took the list. "Thank you, Mr. Bramlett."

"Glad to help."

"Are any of them here today?"

"Gil Thomas and Jeff Plott will be in around ten today, and Kel Dollar's off this morning but should be in by one. Shane McDowell is off today but comes in tomorrow, and Blake Corbin is on vacation until next week."

"We'll be back around ten to talk to Thomas and Plott," Ivy said.

"I'll make sure they're around."

"Oh. One more thing," Ivy said as Bramlett walked them to the door. "Do you cultivate belladonna here at the nursery?"

Bramlett looked puzzled. "No. We don't cultivate toxic medicinals. Too many liability issues."

"Okay, thanks again."

"You're welcome." Bramlett gave a little wave as they headed back to the department-issued Ford Taurus.

Ivy handed Antoine the list of names. "See if we can get addresses and any background on any of these guys before we come back at ten."

"Maybe this is just a big ol' red herring. Shouldn't we start looking at other names on the list, too?"

He was probably right. Nothing about Bramlett Nurseries had pinged her radar. Since they were doing busy-work at the moment, routine stuff, there was no reason they couldn't split up and get the job done twice as fast. "Tell you what. I'll drop you off back at the station so you can start making phone calls. Set up some interviews with the people on the list. I'll come back here and talk to the guys at the nursery, then we can regroup at the end of the day."

"Good idea. We should be able to get through this list in no time if we do it right." Antoine had never been a big fan of down-and-dirty legwork. He liked the puzzle aspect of solving crimes, which made Ivy wonder why he'd stuck around Bitterwood rather than heading for a bigger city, where he'd get more chances to play Sherlock Holmes rather than Barney Fife.

Maybe for the same reason she'd never left Bitterwood. Life in this sleepy mountain town, good or bad, was all she'd ever known. She knew who she was when she was here. She didn't worry about who she could be.

But maybe it was time she expanded her horizons. Maybe it was time to find out who she could be outside of Bitterwood, Tennessee.

And how much of your newfound wanderlust, taunted an inner voice, *comes from knowing that sooner or later, Sutton Calhoun's going to dust this little town off his boots and never look back?*

THE SOUND OF KEYS IN the door roused Sutton from a light slumber. He hadn't bothered with the bed, since Ivy's overstuffed sofa had looked too inviting to pass up, and it was a hell of a lot more comfortable than the hard sofas in the hospital waiting room.

By the time Ivy entered, he was sitting up, shaking off the stupor of sleep. She stopped in the doorway with a soft gasp. "You scared me. What are you doing in here?"

"Napping."

She looked at the sofa dubiously. "Isn't it a little small for you?"

He shook his head, stretching. "Just right." He caught her gaze dropping to his midsection and looked down to see his T-shirt had slipped upward as he stretched, baring his stomach. Amused by catching her staring, he shot her a teasing smile and stood up, taking a deliberate step toward her. "You're home awfully early in the day. Miss me that much?"

Her cheeks turned deliciously pink. "J-just came to pick up some notes I left here." She seemed to have trouble getting the words out past her suddenly tangled tongue. "I, um, I have to go do a couple of interviews soon—"

Amazing, he thought, how the room could heat up so suddenly. He still wasn't touching her, still stood a few feet away, too far from her to even feel the heat of her body radiating toward his, but he would swear he could hear her heart pounding from where he was.

Or was that his own heart he was hearing?

"I did miss you." Her tone was soft. Helpless. He could tell she hadn't meant to say the words, that making herself vulnerable to him with her confession scared the hell out of her.

It scared him, too, because hearing her admission of need sent a wave of pleasure rocketing through him, as powerful as if she'd reached out and touched him.

He wasn't a man who felt things deeply. He didn't let himself, preferring a hard-shelled cocoon of distance and solitude to keep him from getting hurt again. His memories of childhood all shared a common thread of pain, from losing his mother young to learning, revelation by revelation, just what it was his father did to keep food on the table and clothes on his back. He'd watched in silent agony as his friends and their families suffered from his father's sins, hated but understood the inevitable distance that grew between them and him.

Apple didn't fall far from the tree, after all....

"I missed you, too," he admitted, closing the gap between them until he touched her, a light brush of his fingertips against her cheek. "Not just today, either. I missed you when I left. All the time."

She closed her eyes, leaning into his touch. "I figured you'd forgotten me once you had Bitterwood in your rearview mirror."

"I tried. I guess eventually I sort of compartmentalized my life. You know, Bitterwood and everything that came after." He cradled her face between his hands. "Why didn't you tell me about Billy Turlow?"

Her eyes widened, and she pulled away from his grasp. "Who?"

"Seth told me about what Turlow did to you."

She wrapped her arms around her waist, turning her profile to him. "Don't you mean what I did to Billy?"

"Did he rape you?"

She shot him a hard look that made his blood chill. "I never gave him a chance."

He nodded slowly. "Good."

"She wouldn't believe me when I tried to warn her." Ivy's tough expression faltered, and she sank onto the arm of the sofa, hunched forward. "She thought I was making it up to break them up. I told her I wouldn't lie about something like that, but she said I was just jealous of her attention."

"God."

"She just wanted to be happy. She always thinks when she meets a new man that this is the one who's going to make her happy. But she looks for men in all the wrong places."

"What about after you stabbed him?"

"Oh, she believed me then." Ivy shot him a bleak smile. "Kind of hard to wish away the sight of your boyfriend in his jockey shorts lyin' on the floor of your daughter's bedroom with a steak knife sticking out of his ribs."

"How long was it?"

Her eyes narrowed with confusion. "The knife?"

"No. How long after I left town?"

"Oh." She looked down at her feet. "About five months. It was a few days after my sixteenth birthday."

He crossed in front of her, laying his hands on her shoulders. "I'm sorry I wasn't there for you. I'm so sorry."

She shook her head. "What could you have done to stop it?"

"Maybe nothing." He lifted her chin to make her look up at him. "But I'd have been there for you afterward, at least."

"It doesn't matter now. It's done. I'm long past it."

"Are you?" He ran his thumb along the curve of her jaw, noting with a combination of pleasure and fear how her eyelids fluttered shut in response. Pink color rose along her neck, flushed into her cheeks, and he knew she was as vulnerable to the combustive attraction between them as he was.

He could hurt her so easily if he made a mistake.

But could he give her the peace and happiness she deserved?

"I'm not my father, Ivy—"

Her eyes snapped up to meet his. "I never said you were."

"I'm not my father," he repeated. "But I still have some of him in me. I don't always think about how my actions affect other people. I think more about my feelings. How things affect me."

"Most people do."

"I don't want to hurt you. Ever."

She held his gaze a moment, a thoughtful look in her dark eyes. Then she pulled away from him and moved to the window that looked out on the front yard. In profile, she looked more sad than conflicted.

"You said you didn't go to the prom. That was your choice, wasn't it?" he asked, suddenly understanding why she was fighting so hard to keep him at arm's length. "You don't do relationships, right?"

She didn't turn her head. "Right. I date sometimes. I'm not a virgin. But I haven't believed in fairy tales in a long time."

"Because of Billy Turlow?"

She made a soft huff that might have been a laugh. "It didn't take Billy Turlow to cure me of my romantic streak. People come. People go. That's the way of things, more often than not."

He crossed to her side, tucking behind her ear a tendril of hair that had sneaked out of her ponytail. "You're not your mama."

"Close enough. I have a bad habit of wanting things that aren't good for me."

"Do I fall into that category?" He couldn't blame her for thinking so.

She looked up at him. "I don't think you're a grifter like Cleve, but you're not going to stick around forever. Sooner or later, you'll leave. You can be as honorable as they come and it doesn't change anything. You already have one foot out of this town. And I'm planted here like a tree."

He smiled at the description. "Somebody's got to stay around to make sure your mama doesn't get into too much trouble."

"Bitterwood is her home. Hell, the town's been trying

to buy her land for a long time, but she won't budge. She's not going anywhere. And since I'm all she's got—"

He slid his arm around her shoulder and pulled her close, pressing his lips against her forehead. It was meant to be a chaste expression of the friendship they'd once shared, but the feel of her body melting into his proved a potent reminder that he and Ivy Hawkins couldn't be just friends anymore. And apparently, they couldn't afford to be lovers, either.

So where did that leave them?

She pulled away from him. "I've got to talk to a man about a truck."

"Any new leads on that?"

She shook her head. "It's early yet."

He knew she wasn't telling him everything she knew, but he didn't fault her for it. She was walking a thin line between following Rayburn's orders and her own instincts. He didn't want to make things any harder for her.

He walked with her out to the car, catching her hand as she reached to open the door. "I'm going to spend tonight at the hospital with Cleve. The doctor said it was okay, since he's going to need help getting in and out of bed and going to the bathroom."

She squeezed his hand. "That's going to be hard for you, isn't it?"

"I can't get used to seeing him so helpless. He was always the most vibrant, self-possessed person I ever knew." That zest for life had been part of the con man's appeal. He could convince a catfish to buy a raincoat.

"Maybe this will be good in the long run," she suggested. "He'll probably have to do some therapy on that broken arm, and didn't you tell me it was the arm that's mostly useless due to the stroke?"

"So maybe he'll get it right this time instead of being a stubborn cuss?"

She squeezed his hand again before letting it go. "I've got to go."

He caught her chin in his palm and lifted her face, brushing his mouth to hers. Her lips clung for a moment, as if she wanted to prolong the kiss as much as he did. But she pulled away, ducking her head as she opened the car door and slid behind the wheel.

"I guess I may not see you much after this." She didn't look at him, her gaze directed forward as if she had addressed the dashboard instead of him. There was a finality in her voice that he couldn't pretend he didn't hear.

"I had to go, Ivy. If I'd stayed here any longer, it would have killed me. One way or another."

She nodded, still looking forward. "And I have to stay."

"I know." He let the silence linger a moment, then added, "Take care of yourself." He had no other argument to make. She was right. He'd be leaving soon, and she'd be staying, and neither one of them could do a damned thing about it. Prolonging their goodbye would only prolong the pain.

"You take care of yourself, too," she said, her profile frozen in place, as if any expression she might make would cause her to fall apart.

He stepped back, letting her close the car door, and watched her drive away with his heart in his throat. He hadn't managed much of a nap before she came home, and any chance of one now was gone. All that was left to do now was pack up the rest of his things and move on. As usual.

Even if it felt like fifty kinds of wrong.

Chapter Fourteen

"Any luck?"

At the sound of the friendly male voice, Ivy looked up from her cell phone and saw Mark Bramlett standing in an open doorway, a nearly empty pot of coffee in one hand and a cup in the other.

"I'm going to have to verify their alibis, but both of your employees have accounted for the days and times of the murders."

Bramlett smiled. "I could have told you that." He nodded at the coffeepot in his hand. "Would you like a cup of coffee, Detective?"

Considering how much her energy was starting to flag for so early in the day, a cup of coffee sounded like a brilliant idea. "Sure. And is there a room I can borrow while I make a few phone calls?"

"You can do it right here in the break room. I've got to go load the truck for a delivery." He led her into the break room and put a disposable cup in front of her. As he emptied the coffeepot into her cup, he added, "Are you planning to stick around to talk to Kel when he comes in after lunch?"

"I need to make a few calls, and I may end up having to leave for a while," she said. "But if I do, I'll definitely be back this afternoon."

"Cream? Sugar?"

"Two creams, one sugar."

He picked up her cup and crossed to the counter. She took another quick look at her list of messages, unsurprised but nevertheless disappointed that there was nothing from Sutton.

What had she expected, a message begging her to give their relationship a chance? With a wry smile, she set her phone down and turned to accept the coffee from Bramlett. "Thanks."

"You let me know if you need anything." With a small wave, he left the break room, closing the door behind him.

Waiting for the coffee to cool, she called Antoine to check on his progress. He sounded a little out of breath when he answered.

"I've never walked so many hills in my life," he complained. "Next job I take, it's going to be somewhere like Kansas. Nice and flat."

"Anything suspicious about any of the trucks?"

"Well, half of 'em looked like they hadn't been washed in years, so I don't think they're going to be our mystery trucks. I'm looking into the alibis on a couple that might fit the bill, but nothing about those truck operators struck me as particularly suspicious. Any luck at the nursery?"

"Not yet. I'm going to make some calls from here, maybe stick around and talk to the employee who's coming in at one unless something comes up."

"All right. I'll let you know if I come across anything on my end. You do the same?"

"You bet." Ivy hung up and pulled out her notepad to check her interview notes. Next call, Plott's pastor, since Plott swore he'd been at church helping out on a mission project the night Amelia Sanderson was killed. But when she dialed the number he'd given her, she got a voice mail message informing her everyone was out to lunch. She left a message for the pastor to call her and picked up the cup of coffee, starting to take a sip.

She paused just before the coffee touched her lips.

Slowly, she lowered the cup back to the table and looked down at the milky-brown liquid. Two creams, one sugar, just as she'd requested. But had she actually watched Bramlett put the extras in her coffee?

She looked behind her at the counter. Two torn individual creamer packets and a sugar packet ripped in two lay on the counter. She crossed to the counter to examine them, feeling ridiculously paranoid. But if their theory was correct, the person who'd killed their four victims had also planted the belladonna at the cemetery. And a single belladonna leaf contained enough poison to kill an adult human.

How hard would it be to infuse a cup of coffee with crushed belladonna leaves? Or put a tasteless, colorless drug like Rohypnol in her drink while she had her back turned?

She started to leave the cup of coffee where it sat, then thought better of it and poured the liquid down the drain of the break room sink. She pulled a pair of latex gloves from her pocket, picked up the empty cup and pulled off the glove, letting it turn inside out and envelop the cup. After tying the wrist opening into a knot, she placed the cup into her purse and dropped back into the chair in front of the table, feeling equal parts stupid and relieved.

A knock on the break room door made her jump. Mark Bramlett stood in the doorway, an apologetic smile on his face. "Sorry to interrupt, but I just came across something kind of strange on the underside of the truck. Would you come take a look and tell me if I'm just imagining things?"

Curiosity eclipsed her paranoia, and she followed Bramlett out of the office. There was nobody else in the front office, she noted with surprise, not even the two men she'd just interviewed. Maybe they were all out in the greenhouses, she supposed, walking fast to keep up with Bramlett's long-legged stride.

"I wouldn't have even seen it at all if I hadn't thought I heard something under the truck. Occasionally a possum or raccoon, or even a feral cat, will crawl up into the underside of vehicles to get warm. I didn't want to start the truck and chop some poor critter into pieces. So I looked up under the truck and I spotted something under the back axle."

He waved his hand toward the back wheels, as if giving her permission to take a look.

She crouched beside the wheel and bent lower, sticking her head under the truck to see what he was talking about.

Suddenly, she felt something grab her shoulder and jerk her upward, slamming her head into the underside of the truck. Pain exploded in the back of her head, stealing her breath. Her vision swam a moment, specks of light dancing in an undulating kaleidoscope of color and darkness.

She was being dragged backward, like a rag doll, and for a moment, she couldn't understand what was happening. Why wasn't she fighting? Shouldn't she be fighting back?

Her vision cleared enough for her to see that she was moving around the bumper to the open doors at the back of the truck. The hands that were still holding her hauled her up into the truck box, shoving her face down onto the hard floor.

She tried to move, her hand flailing for her service pistol. It was ripped from her before she got a good grip, and she growled a profanity, trying to roll over onto her back. Bramlett's face swam into view, his expression hard and businesslike.

She kicked out at him, but the effort earned her a hard smack to the jaw, knocking her back into the truck. He ran his hands over her suit jacket and trousers in a rough search. "Where is it?"

"What?"

He closed his hand around her neck, compressing her trachea until she couldn't breathe without wheezing. "Your cell phone. Where is it?"

She clawed at his hands and he hit her again. There was something she should be doing. She'd learned things about protecting herself even from a bigger attacker, but the details slogged out of reach, somewhere in the muddy mists of her aching brain.

He let go of her and backed out of the truck. She found the strength to launch herself after him, but she ended up slamming face-first into the back doors of the truck. There was no handle on the inside, only a smooth, solid wall of nothing where the door should be.

Her legs felt like noodles, helpless to keep her on her feet. She slithered into a weak puddle in front of the locked door, banging her hand against the door more in frustration than any hope that someone might hear her and let her out.

The truck's engine growled to life, and suddenly they were moving, the forward lurch knocking her into the door again. Flattening her hands against the floor, she steadied herself until she felt confident she wouldn't fall over again anytime soon. Her fuzzy head was starting to clear, the pain from her knock in the head subsiding from a howl to a low roar.

But she was still locked in the back of a truck driven by a man she was becoming utterly certain must be the killer they were seeking.

And God only knew what would happen once the truck stopped.

He shouldn't call her. She'd made her decision clear enough that morning, in her stubborn refusal to meet his gaze as they said what had felt like a final goodbye.

But the phone felt heavy in his pocket as he pulled into a parking slot in front of Ledbetter's Diner, a visceral reminder that he still had a choice. She'd made it clear she wasn't going to leave Bitterwood as long as her mother was still there. And he'd vowed a long time ago that he'd never come back to this place again. Certainly not for good.

But he could change his mind. Or she could change hers. Anything seemed possible now that the only alternative was walking away from Ivy Hawkins forever.

She made him feel centered. Connected to something. He'd let himself forget that she'd always had that effect on him, even when they were little more than two scared, lonely kids looking for someone to trust. He'd let himself walk away all those years ago. He'd left her behind to fend for herself, cut that cord between them. He'd let himself forget how much that severed connection had bled during those first scary, lonely days on his own.

It would bleed again if he left her behind.

Damn it, he didn't want to feel this much again. He'd gotten good at not feeling much at all, just the light buzz of camaraderie with his fellow soldiers, the respect and admiration he had for the people he now worked with at Cooper Security. It made life easier to deal with, less messy and constrained.

Less alive.

Well, now he was alive. And it ached like a son of a bitch. But he didn't think he could trade it for numbness again.

He pulled out his cell phone and dialed her number, waiting with his heart in his throat. After three rings with no answer, he realized she might just be ignoring his call.

Maybe he should take that as her answer.

Then someone picked up. A male voice. "Yeah?"

The unfamiliar voice gave him a start. "I—I must have the wrong number—"

"Maybe not," the voice on the other end said. "I just found this cell phone on the ground. Maybe whoever you're calling lost it?"

Sutton felt a flutter of unease. "Where are you?"

"Bramlett Nurseries in Bitterwood, Tennessee."

Ivy had been going to see a man about a truck. Had Bramlett Nurseries been one of the names on her list? If it was, she might have found the place of particular interest because of the deadly nightshade plants. After all, where better to look for a plant than at a nursery? "I was calling Detective Ivy Hawkins with the Bitterwood Police Department."

"Oh, yeah!" the man on the other end of the phone said. "Yeah, I seen her earlier, talking to the boss. Reckon maybe she just dropped it by accident. Want me to see if I can find her around here?"

"That would be great."

There was the muffled sound of movement on the other end of the call, muted voices conferring just out of earshot. Finally the man said, "She was definitely here a few minutes ago, but nobody knows where she is now."

"Okay, thanks." He started to hang up, then added, "Hey, you still there?"

"Yes, sir."

"Where are you located?"

"Emerson Valley, just outside Bitterwood. If you've been 'round here long, there used to be a horse farm where we are now—Emerson Farm? Used to raise Tennessee walkers."

"I know the place. Thanks."

Emerson Valley was only about ten minutes away. He

made it there in eight minutes and parked next to Ivy's department car, which sat near the front entrance of the sprawling plant nursery.

There was a man at the front counter, finishing up with a customer. Sutton waited, looking around for Ivy inside the store, but she wasn't in sight.

When he got the chance to talk to the clerk, he introduced himself, grimacing inwardly at the man's wary shift in expression when he said the name "Calhoun." "I called earlier, looking for Detective Hawkins."

"Right. Yeah, we haven't found her yet."

Sutton frowned. "Her car's still parked outside."

"Oh." The man looked surprised. "I just figured she left when the boss left."

"The boss?"

"Mr. Bramlett. He took off in the truck about fifteen minutes ago."

"Could Detective Hawkins have gone with him?"

The man shook his head. "I don't think so. Mr. Bramlett was by himself when he drove off."

Fingers of alarm crept up Sutton's spine. "You're sure?"

"Yeah, I saw him go. Just him in the driver's seat. I didn't see nobody else with him, which I thought was kind of weird 'cause he was hauling a big mulch order over to the park in Meadowbrook—you don't want to try to handle that by yourself."

"He didn't take the mulch order." A man passing by stopped and laid his hand on the counter. "Mulch order's still out there on the loading dock."

"Oh." Once again the man behind the counter looked flummoxed. "Okay, then."

"Can you call Mr. Bramlett?" Sutton asked.

"Sure thing." The counterman pulled a phone receiver from beneath the counter and punched in a number. He waited a few seconds, then looked up at Sutton. "No answer. That's odd."

Very odd, Sutton thought, his gut starting to tighten. "Were you the one who found her cell phone?"

"No, that was Kel." The counterman called over a man in grimy jeans and a faded denim shirt with the words *Bramlett Nurseries* embroidered on the left front pocket. "You found that phone, right?"

"That's right," Kel answered. He looked with curiosity at Sutton.

"Can you show me where you found it?" Sutton asked.

"Yeah, sure." Kel led him outside, past the loading dock, where several pallets full of packaged mulch sat, and stopped in a grass-free area a few yards away. "It was layin' right here."

Sutton scanned the area for any sign of Ivy. He didn't see her, but he spotted fresh-looking tire tracks in the soft ground. "Is this where you park the company truck?"

"Sometimes. It was parked there this morning, anyway."

All the pieces were starting to fall into place, and the picture they formed had Sutton's heart rattling hard against his sternum. "Thanks," he told Kel, walking a few feet away and getting into his truck. He dug Ivy's business card from his wallet. Her cell phone number was most prominent, but there was a Bitterwood Police Department direct-line number in smaller print under the address. He gave it a call and asked for Antoine Parsons.

Unfortunately, it wasn't Antoine who answered. "Mr. Calhoun." It took only a second for Sutton to place the voice. Glen Rayburn. He had a particularly smarmy way of saying the name "Calhoun."

"Captain Rayburn, I'm looking for Ivy Hawkins. I have reason to believe she may be in danger."

"Oh, she's in danger, son. Of losing her job if she keeps

fraternizing with unsavory characters. I'll be sure to mention your call to her." Rayburn hung up on him.

Son of a bitch! Sutton pulled up the number he'd saved for Davenport Trucking and dialed the main number. "Rachel Davenport, please," he said when the receptionist answered.

"Ms. Davenport is out this morning," the receptionist replied.

"Then Mr. Davenport."

"He's with Ms. Davenport."

Damn it. "Listen, I have reason to believe one of your trucks is being used to commit crimes. I assume you have a GPS tracker on all your trucks?"

"Yes, sir," the woman said, "but we don't track them as a policy. We only check the GPS information if there's a billing discrepancy or some sort of legal issue."

"Murder *is* a legal issue!" Sutton snapped.

"Murder?" The woman stuttered the word.

"Three of your previous employees are dead, and this truck may be involved in the killings."

The woman's voice took on a distinctly wary tone. "Sir, if this is some sort of prank call, please stop. We will report you to the authorities." She hung up on him.

He slammed his hand against the steering wheel. The blow stung all the way up his arm, but he held on to the sensation, used the pain to center himself. There was one option left. Not a great one, but he had to take a chance. He dialed another number.

On the third ring, Seth Hammond answered. "Sutton? Is something wrong with Cleve?"

"No, he's doing fine. Flirting with nurses when I left him."

Seth chuckled. "That's about right."

"Listen, I hate asking you this, but time may be running out." As economically as he could, he told Seth what he suspected. "Bramlett was on a list of companies renting trucks from Davenport at the time of the murders."

"And you think someone there might be the killer?" Seth sounded skeptical. "Just because of the connection to Davenport?"

"It's not that simple, but I can't explain it."

"'Cause God knows, I ain't trustworthy, right, Sutton?"

"I've already trusted you with more than I probably ought to," Sutton shot back. "I need your help, Seth. Is there any way to access real-time tracking of the GPS units in those trucks?"

"Yeah, we've done it before to help the police find one of our stolen units," Seth said. "But management will require a warrant, I'm pretty sure."

"I don't have time for that. I think the man who killed those four women may have Ivy Hawkins."

"Just because she lost her phone?"

It wasn't that simple, but Sutton didn't know how to explain his certainty without sounding like a fool. Something was wrong. Ivy was in trouble. He knew it bone deep. "If we were ever friends, Seth, help me."

Seth was silent a moment. "There's a way to access the GPS, but I may have to tell a few lies to get it done."

Sutton bit back a desperate laugh. "You ought to be able to handle that. Don't you think?"

"Yeah, I reckon I can. Do you know the unit number?"

"No. But it's the truck that Bramlett Nurseries rents."

"Okay. Let me see what I can do. I'll call you back."

"Soon, Seth. It's gotta be soon."

"The mighty Sutton Calhoun. Knocked to his knees by a little bitty girl." Seth's taunting murmur lacked bite. "I'll hurry." He hung up.

Sutton pressed his head against the steering wheel, hoping time hadn't already run out.

Five minutes later, his cell phone rang. "Old Lumber Mill Road, about a mile south of the turnoff to Townsend Road." Seth Hammond's voice greeted him without preamble. "It's been stationary for five minutes."

A jolt of pure adrenaline zapped Sutton's nervous system. "Thanks."

"You want me to call the cops?" Seth asked.

"Call Antoine Parsons—remember him from high school? Tell him Ivy may be in danger and where we think she is."

"He's not going to believe me."

"Make him." Sutton hung up and put the truck in gear.

THE DIZZINESS HAD GONE, along with most of the ache in Ivy's head. She'd ended up bleeding quite a bit from the gash in her scalp, but she'd stanched the flow with her suit jacket. The wound had settled down to a slow ooze instead of a gush. But that was the end of the good news. She was still stuck in the back of the locked truck, still forced to sit in one place to keep from being pitched around by the vehicle's motion.

She took advantage of every time the truck stopped moving to feel her way around the truck box, trying to remember the details of the interior from her brief inspection earlier that morning.

Had it been only that morning? Somehow, her first trip to Bramlett Nurseries felt as if it had happened a lifetime ago.

The truck stopped again, and she pushed to her feet, resuming her tactile search of the truck box. She came across a loose bit of metal batten covering a seam and plucked at it with her fingers. It gave as she pulled, and she jerked harder. The strip tore away from the box. "Yes!" she breathed.

The piece of batten wasn't long, as it seemed to have covered only a short seam, and she could have hoped for something a little more substantial than a ruler-thin strip of flexible metal to use as a weapon. But it was better than nothing, and a moment later, when the engine died away and she realized they had parked, she was glad to have it.

It was short enough to conceal behind her back, she realized, tucking it into the waistband of her trousers. It lay flat against her spine, the top of the batten resting against her neck. As long as she didn't turn around to give Bramlett a look at her back, she could use it as a weapon if she needed it.

She heard the rattle of the lock on the back door and braced herself for a fight. The door opened, letting in a blinding amount of light. She slid into the corner at the back, praying for her eyesight to adjust quickly.

Bramlett's silhouette filled the doorway, bigger than she remembered. She wondered if that's how he'd appeared to his previous victims, faceless death, too powerful and relentless to defeat.

To hell with that. She might go down, but not without giving the bastard a damned good fight.

"You killed the other women." As her eyes adjusted to the flow of light, she began to make out his features. Her words made him smile, and he clapped slowly.

"Brava, Detective. You figured it out."

"Clearly, you knew I would. Since you took the stupid chance of kidnapping me from your very own nursery."

He shrugged. "I'm done here, once I take care of you and one more little bit of unfinished business."

"Business? I'm not buying that." The strip of batten felt ridiculously insubstantial where it lay against her spine, but she refused to let any hint of defeat creep in. "You enjoy killing. It shows in your handiwork."

"I do. I really do." Bramlett's smile widened. "But it *is* business. I've been paid well to do what I did."

"By whom?"

He shook his head. "No big confessions from the killer, Detective. This isn't a movie, and you're not going to live to tell the tale anyway."

In a flash, so fast she barely had time to react, he threw himself at her. And it was only in that last second, as she whipped the strip of batten from behind her back, that she caught the glimmer of light on the blade of a deadly-looking hunting knife in his right hand.

Chapter Fifteen

If there was a truck parked on the side of Old Lumber Mill Road, it wasn't readily apparent. Sutton pulled his truck onto the shoulder of the road at the mile marker and tried not to panic.

Had Seth screwed up the GPS tracking? He reached for his phone and started to dial Seth's number when he spotted the flash of white barely visible through a stand of poplar trees just off the road. A light breeze was making the leaves and limbs dance, revealing what looked like the side of a white box truck mostly hidden from view several yards off the shoulder.

Sutton checked the Glock's ammunition and got out of the truck, trying to move as silently as possible. The crunch of gravel beneath his feet led him quickly off the shoulder and onto the grass beyond. There wasn't much of a drop-off from the shoulder to the ground, which would have made it easy for the truck to leave the road and move into seclusion.

The ground was a little uneven, complicating his attempt to make a steady approach without risking discovery, but Sutton had spent the first eighteen years of his life exploring the woods and mountains around Bitterwood. Just a mile through these woods was the base of the ridge where he'd lived. Where Ivy had lived as well, in a shabby little two-bedroom bungalow her mother had tried to keep clean and decorated despite their limited resources.

Ivy had bitterly insisted her mother's industry was more about attracting a man than making a good life for herself and her daughter, but Sutton thought now, with time and distance, that Arlene Hendry had been doing the best she could for her daughter, as well.

From where he now stood, he had a pretty good view of the side of the truck. The back doors stood open, and the box trailer seemed to be rocking.

He crept closer, drawing near enough to confirm that something was happening inside the trailer box. He heard a grunt of pain, faint but unmistakable. It sounded masculine, but it was followed shortly by a sharp, feminine cry.

Heart in his throat, he raced toward the truck.

UP CLOSE, THE BATTEN was proving to be a poor weapon, but it was doing a creditable job as a shield, helping her deflect Mark Bramlett's vicious stabs with the hunting knife. Clearheaded and prepared, she was making far better use of her self-defense training, turning her smaller size into an asset as she dodged and ducked, striking sharp, swift blows with her feet and fists to the vulnerable spots on his body.

She saw an opening and struck, whipping the batten through the air and slicing a jagged tear in his left cheek, knocking him off balance. As he stumbled backward into the side of the truck box, she sprang toward the open back door. She almost made it out the doors before Bramlett hit her from behind. Pain exploded in her right shoulder, making her cry out, and they both tumbled out of the truck. Bramlett landed on top of her and bounced off, but the hard contact with the ground robbed Ivy of her chance to run. She gasped for breath, trying to push to her feet. She made it halfway before Bramlett slammed into her again, knocking her into the back wheel of the truck. He pinned her there, raising the knife in a swinging arc.

And then, with shocking suddenness, he was gone.

It took a second for Ivy's swimming vision to clear enough to take in the violent struggle going on a few feet away from her. Sutton's broad back flexed as he fought to pin Bramlett's knife hand to the ground.

Bramlett's knee came up, aimed between Sutton's legs. Sutton was able to deflect part of the blow, but Bramlett's knee continued upward, slamming into Sutton's gut, eliciting an explosive grunt of pain. His left leg buckled, knocking him off balance, and he tumbled sideways onto the ground, pulling Mark Bramlett with him.

The shift in position gave Bramlett a sudden edge, and he took it, whipping the knife in a slashing arc toward Sutton's neck.

Ivy launched herself at Bramlett, grabbing his knife hand before it could land the blow. The blade slashed into Sutton's upper arm, blood blooming red across his torn shirtsleeve, a flesh wound instead of a mortal blow. Ivy clung to Bramlett's arm as he tried to swing her off, only letting go when his elbow slammed into her solar plexus, making her vision dance with alternating spots of darkness and glittering stars.

She had the terrifying impression of death itself rising up, stinking of the grave, looming over her with deadly intent. The glitter of a blade, a lethal arc slicing through the air.

Then a loud crack and death disintegrated into a crumpled body that landed at her feet, mortally human.

Mark Bramlett's gray eyes locked with hers. His mouth moved as if he was trying to form words. He had taken a bullet in the lower chest and blood was spreading fast, already drenching the front of his golf shirt.

A few feet away, Sutton still held his Glock in a firing stance, his gaze locked on Bramlett's body, ready to move if the man made one more move toward Ivy.

But Bramlett wasn't going anywhere. He was bleeding out, fast. There would be no way to get medical help here in time to save him.

"Who hired you?" Ivy found her breath and crawled toward him on her hands and knees. With the side of her hand, she swept away the knife he'd dropped, knocking it out of reach.

The sound of running footsteps behind them drew her attention away from Bramlett for a moment. She saw Seth Hammond jog to a halt a few feet away from where Bramlett lay. His green eyes were wide with dismay at the sight of Bramlett's bleeding body.

He pushed past Sutton, who put out a hand to stop him, and crouched next to Ivy, his attention focused solely on Mark Bramlett. "Why her?"

Ivy grabbed Seth's arm, tugging him away. "Get out of my crime scene."

"He targeted Rachel Davenport," Seth snapped. "It's the only thing that makes sense. I want to know why."

"I want to know who," Ivy shot back, turning to look at the dying man. "Who hired you, Bramlett?"

Bramlett's mouth stretched into a horrible grin. Blood bubbled on his lips as he gasped for breath. "He's right. It's all about the girl."

His voice faded into a guttural rattle, and blood filled his mouth, spilling down his chin and onto the ground. His eyes twitched for a second, then went dead, his eyelids sliding half-shut.

"Son of a bitch!" Seth growled, lurching forward as if to

grab the body by the shoulders. Sutton wrapped his arms around him in a bear hug and pulled him away.

Ivy felt for a carotid pulse. It was silent.

She looked up at Sutton, who still held Seth away from the body, and shook her head.

"Are you okay?" he asked.

She hurt all over, especially on the back of her right shoulder, where a wet spot was forming, suggesting that at least one of Bramlett's knife blows had hit its mark. "I think he got me in the back, but I'm okay."

"Stay put," Sutton warned Seth and let the other man go, hurrying over to Ivy's side. He examined her shoulder, plucking at the wet fabric. "Are all the muscles and tendons moving okay?"

She tried rolling her shoulder. It hurt, but everything seemed to work the way it was supposed to. "How about your arm?"

"Flesh wound," he answered shortly. "Your head is bloody."

"He banged my head into the underside of the truck to subdue me at first," she said flatly. "I didn't lose consciousness." Not fully, anyway. "It's stopped bleeding, hasn't it?"

"You shouldn't have killed him," Seth muttered.

Sutton's head whipped around to look at the other man. "If I hadn't, he'd have killed Ivy."

"You heard him. It's all about Rachel Davenport." Seth sounded oddly desperate. "He knew who's targeting her."

Ivy couldn't argue with Seth. She was pretty sure Rachel Davenport had been the target all along. Someone had hired Bramlett to kill people around her rather than kill her outright. But what had been the point? What were they trying to do, rip away her friends and support system? To what end? Even though she now knew the identity of the killer, knew that someone had hired him to commit the murders, and even knew that it was all about Rachel Davenport, she was as frustrated as ever.

"What's it to you?" Sutton asked suspiciously.

Seth's expression shifted into neutral. "I work for Davenport Trucking. What happens to the people there affects me."

Not even Seth looked as if he could sell that load of bull, but Ivy didn't see the point of pushing him. There was too much else to take care of. "We've got to call in backup."

"I got hold of Antoine Parsons on my way here." Seth rose and walked a few feet away. "He should be here any minute."

Ivy's legs had begun to tremble. She sat down with her back pressed against the truck tire, looking away from Bramlett's body to lock gazes with Sutton. He stared back at her, his eyes burning like coals. The intensity of his gaze scorched through her until she had to look away to catch her breath.

Distant sirens wafted in on the soft midday breeze. The cavalry was on the way, Ivy thought, closing her eyes and resting her head against the tire. Pain throbbed in her scalp, reminding her of her head wound, as well.

"Ivy?" Sutton's voice was sharp with alarm.

"Just resting my eyes," she said, forcing her heavy lids open.

He was crouched closer than she expected, filling her view. He blocked out everything else, and she realized with weary bemusement that he'd been doing so ever since he walked back into her life a few days ago. She'd been consumed by him, even when she was working her case. She'd let him get under her skin again, against all good sense, and she had a feeling she'd be paying for that mistake for the rest of her life.

Because he still had one foot out of town, especially

now that the case he'd come to investigate had more or less been solved.

It wouldn't be long before the rest of him followed.

"ALL DONE." THE E.R. doctor stitching the cut on Sutton's upper arm was young, female and impossibly cheery. Antoine had convinced Ivy to let an ambulance take her to River Bend Medical Center in Knoxville. Sutton had followed in his truck, but since nobody in the emergency department would let him see Ivy until they'd finished examining her, he had given in and let them patch up his wound while he waited.

Seth had disappeared at some point before the police arrived. Sutton supposed he hadn't wanted any unnecessary encounters with the law. He was curious about the other man's reaction to Mark Bramlett's death—Seth had looked downright distraught when he realized Bramlett wouldn't be able to answer any of his questions about Rachel Davenport.

What the hell was going on there? Sutton doubted Rachel Davenport even knew who Seth Hammond was. He was just some guy who worked in the fleet garage. If she ran into him more than once or twice a week, it would probably be a fluke. So why did he care who had hired Bramlett to kill the people around her? Was it simply because someone had tried to hire Seth to do it himself?

Another mystery, he thought, his lips curving slightly as the doctor finished applying a bandage over his stitches. Another excuse to stick around Bitterwood a little bit longer.

Maybe even for good.

His cell phone rang, drawing a furrowed brow from the doctor. "We really don't want people using their cells in the examining area."

He looked at the display. Jesse Cooper. He'd already

missed three calls from his boss. What was one more? He pocketed the phone and smiled at the doctor, who smiled back with approval. "I can go now?"

"Follow up with your own doctor in a few days."

He left the small emergency bay and went looking for Ivy. A nurse shooed him back out to the waiting area, where he ran into Antoine.

"Have you seen her yet?" he asked as Sutton sat down in the chair beside him and pulled out his phone.

"Not yet. Should we worry that it's taking so long?"

"I don't know." Antoine's brow furrowed deeply. "She said she didn't lose consciousness, but no way in hell Bramlett hustles her into the truck without a fight unless she was at least a little woozy."

That was Sutton's worry, as well. Head wounds were unpredictable. Little bumps on the head could lead to lethal brain bleeds. To distract himself from his worry, he asked, "Anything new on Bramlett's motives?"

While Sutton had been undergoing questions from the police before he'd been released to seek treatment for his arm, nobody in the Bitterwood Police Department had seemed willing to speculate about why a friendly, seemingly good-natured businessman had decided to take a contract killing job and pursue it with such apparent zest. In fact, based on some of the early hostility he'd faced until all the facts settled into place, it seemed the police were more inclined to see him as the suspect and Bramlett as the victim.

"I got an interesting report from the Nashville police right before I got the call about Ivy's abduction," Antoine told him, lowering his voice. Sutton supposed that, technically, Antoine shouldn't be sharing information with a civilian. But Sutton didn't feel like just any old civilian. He'd come close to losing Ivy at the point of Mark Bramlett's knife. He wanted to know how he'd hidden his murderous side so long.

"Interesting how?" he asked.

"Until last year, the Nashville P.D. was looking for a serial killer who'd been killing women in their own homes. They think the killer stalked his victims, figured out when they'd be alone at night and attacked when they had been asleep in bed for a few hours."

"Let me guess. Bramlett spent some time in Nashville."

"Lived there until his uncle died and left him the nursery here in Bitterwood. He moved here a year ago—"

"And the Nashville murders stopped?"

"Looks that way. Nashville thinks they may be able to match his DNA if Bramlett's their killer. I've already arranged for TBI to handle the evidence transfer."

"These murders here in Bitterwood weren't random serial killings," Sutton said firmly. "Whoever paid Bramlett to kill those women may have lucked into a bona fide serial killer as a hired gun, but those women are dead for a specific reason, and Ivy and I both think it has something to do with Rachel Davenport."

Antoine looked thoughtful but didn't respond, and a moment later, Sutton's cell phone rang, dragging his attention away. It was Jesse Cooper, calling back. With a frown, he got up and went to an empty corner of the waiting room to answer. "Calhoun."

"Where the hell have you been?" Jesse asked, dispensing with polite greetings. "I've been trying to call you for over an hour."

"I was closing a case," Sutton answered drily. "Something up?"

"Emergency case in northern Iraq. Four employees of Campelli Construction working on projects in the Kurdish region have been taken hostage in a standoff between the

Turkish military and the Kongra-Gel rebels. You're one of our only operatives who speak both Turkish and Kurdish. We need you on the ground helping out with negotiations so we can end this without losing any Campelli employees."

"How soon?" Sutton's heart sank.

"We're sending the chopper up to Bitterwood to get you. Should be there within an hour. Delilah's aboard—she'll take over your case."

"I'm in Knoxville," he said bleakly, "and our part of the case is closed. We know who killed April Billings." He caught Jesse up as tersely as possible, his stomach aching with dismay.

How could he leave here in a matter of hours? He had so much he hadn't had a chance to say to Ivy, so much he wanted to ask her. To offer her. Hell, he couldn't even be sure she'd be through in the E.R. before he had to go.

"You'll have to go back to Bitterwood to get your things, I guess. Can you get there and get packed up within an hour?" Jesse asked. "J.D.'s going to set the chopper down at some place called Hardy's Field. Said it's in the valley near the lumberyard?"

"I know it," Sutton said, wanting off the phone now. He needed to talk to Ivy before he left. He had to make her see that this time, he wasn't abandoning her again. He would be back. Nothing short of death itself would keep him from coming back to her.

"Delilah can do the follow-up with Billings and close out the case," Jesse said. "You better get a move on. You've got to make a flight out of Atlanta to JFK in four hours."

"I need more than an hour," he told Jesse. "My father's in the hospital—I can't leave without seeing him. And I need to check on the cop who got injured—"

"Okay, two hours. That's the best I can do. You've got a limited amount of time to get on that plane to JFK."

"Fine. Two hours. I'll make it work."

"Problems?" Antoine was walking back to his chair as Sutton returned. He had two cups of coffee and handed one to Sutton.

"I have to leave for Atlanta by chopper in two hours. I've got to see both my father and Ivy before I go. Any word on her?"

"I checked while you were on the phone. Last word is that she's been sent for a CAT scan."

Sutton's heart dropped. "They think her head injury is that bad?"

"I get the feeling it's mainly a precaution. But she could be here at least another hour, best-case scenario." Antoine looked apologetic. "You really have to go so quickly?"

"The job requires my skill set," he answered vaguely. "Any way to get me in to see her before I have to leave?"

"Captain Rayburn himself is waiting to see her, swinging his shield around like a great big—" Antoine flashed a brief but wicked grin. "Anyway, if nobody's letting him in, they're not going to let you in, either."

So that was it, Sutton thought. If he was going to meet the chopper and make the plane, he'd have to leave in the next hour. If they didn't let anyone see her before then, he'd have to leave without talking to her.

At least he had to go back to her house to get the rest of his things. He could leave her a note, try to say in writing what he wouldn't get a chance to say in person.

But it wouldn't be enough.

"You have a visitor," the nurse told Ivy as she came into the narrow emergency bay to check her vitals. They were waiting for final word from the CAT scan, but Ivy knew it would be normal. Her head wasn't even hurting anymore, and now that they'd stitched up her shoulder wound and cleaned up the split skin of her scalp, she was feeling more like herself.

And now, finally, she was going to get to see Sutton and make sure he'd fared as well from their ordeal. She ran her fingers through her tangled hair, trying to comb it into some semblance of order, and smiled as the curtains parted to admit her visitor.

But it wasn't Sutton. It was Captain Rayburn.

"I told you to keep Sutton Calhoun out of your investigation. So you can imagine my surprise when I hear he's shot and killed our prime suspect."

"He saved my life."

"He shouldn't have been there at all."

She stared at the captain. "You do realize that if he hadn't been there, I'd be dead now."

For a moment, Rayburn looked chastised. But his expression hardened immediately. "You're on paid administrative leave pending a full investigation of the incident. We've recovered your weapon from the truck, so no need to turn that in. You're damned lucky it wasn't used to kill you."

"Clearly he preferred killing with his knife," she muttered, anger boiling in her gut.

"I'll call you with the details of your performance hearing." Rayburn stared back at her, satisfaction shining in his eyes. He'd wanted her out all along, and this time, it looked as if he had a chance of getting his way without bringing the diversity police down on his head.

But why? What had she done to earn his antagonism? Was it just because she was a woman? Or was there something else going on?

A few minutes later, the doctor came in, wearing a careful smile. "All good news on your tests. I think we're safe to let you go home now."

"Oh, wow. Faster than I expected." She'd have to hunt Sutton down so he could give her a ride home.

But when she walked out to the waiting room to find him, only Antoine was there. He looked up at her with a big grin. "They're springing you?"

"Already sprung. Just looking for a ride home."

"Got you covered, Hawk." He rose to his feet and pulled her into a big hug, careful with her bandaged shoulder. He lowered his voice a little. "Did Rayburn ever get in to see you?"

She grimaced. "Yeah."

Antoine's grin disappeared. "What's going on?"

"He wants me out. Maybe he's going to get it this time. I'm on paid administrative leave." She looked around. "Is Sutton still being examined?" A hint of alarm buzzed through her nervous system. Had he been more injured than he'd let on?

"He didn't get in to see you, then?" Something in Antoine's voice made her gut tighten.

"No. Why?"

"He had to leave the hospital, but he was hoping to see you first."

She stared at him, not following. "I thought he gave his statement about the shooting at the scene. Is Rayburn going to give him trouble about it? It was a legit shooting, Antoine. I'd be dead if he hadn't fired."

"No, we gave him the okay to leave town. We've got his contact information if we need to follow up."

She stared at him. "Leave town?"

Antoine took her hand, giving it a light squeeze. "He got a call from his boss. They've sent a chopper to take him to the airport in Atlanta. He's got a new assignment out of the country."

Chapter Sixteen

Cleve stared back at Sutton, unblinking, as he explained he had to leave town again. "I don't know that you give a damn anyway," Sutton said with a rueful smile. "But I'm glad I got to see you. I'm going to stay in touch this time, whether you like it or not. 'Cause it's a sin and a disgrace for a man to leave his father's well-being to the likes of Seth Hammond."

"I heard that," said the man whose footsteps Sutton had heard coming.

Sutton turned to look at Seth. He'd lost that frantic look he'd had earlier in the woods, and he'd changed clothes, out of his work coveralls and into a long-sleeved T-shirt and a pair of jeans. At a glance, he almost looked like the boy Sutton remembered from all those years ago, all long legs, green eyes and a feral cat grin.

"So you're leavin' again?" Seth asked.

"A job came up overseas. I'm one of the only people at the agency fluent in the two languages involved."

"Well, hell. I'd just got used to seein' your ugly face around these parts." Seth walked closer and held out his hand.

Sutton stood and shook the other man's hand. "I hope you were telling the truth about turning over a new leaf. Because I plan to be coming around here a lot more often."

"I get the feelin' it ain't me and your old man you'll be comin' here to see."

Sutton smiled but didn't answer. He turned back to his father's bedside and found the old man looking at him with thoughtful eyes. "You got something to say, Cleve?"

His father's mouth slowly formed words. "Don't…be…a stranger." He let go of a big whoosh of breath and grinned.

"Sure, talk up a storm for the pretty boy," Seth grumbled. But his eyes were smiling.

"I've got to get my stuff together so I can meet the helicopter. They should be landing in Bitterwood in about sixty minutes." Sutton looked at his father. "I expect you out of this bed and doing therapy by the time I get back. Understand, old man?"

Cleve's answer was profane, but he was grinning the whole time.

"Take care of him," Sutton told Seth as the other man walked him out into the corridor.

"I'll do my best. You be careful over there, wherever you're going. Say hi to Dee if you see her."

"She's coming to do the mop-up on these murders, actually," Sutton said, remembering what Jesse had told him. "You'll get to see her yourself."

He couldn't tell if Seth was pleased by the news or not, but he didn't have time to figure it out. He was running out of time to see Ivy before he had to leave.

But when he checked with the emergency-room admitting nurse, she told him Ivy had already left the hospital. "She left with a tall black man about fifteen minutes ago."

Damn it! If she was with Antoine, that meant she knew he was leaving town. She probably thought he'd hightailed it out of Tennessee once again without even telling her goodbye.

He pulled out his cell phone and started to call hers

when he remembered her phone was still at Bramlett Nurseries. He shoved the phone back in his pocket with a growl and jogged out to the visitor parking area. Fortunately, his gas tank was half-full, which would get him back to Bitterwood with no problem.

But would Ivy be willing to meet him halfway once he got there?

THERE WAS AN OLD, powder-blue Ford Mustang convertible parked in the driveway when Antoine pulled his car to a stop in front of Ivy's house. He shot her an apologetic look. "I thought I should call your mother and let her know what was going on. I told her there wasn't any need to come to the hospital until we knew if you'd be staying, but—"

Ivy shook her head. "No problem." Right now, she thought, she could probably use a hug from her mother.

Arlene had swept the floors and dusted the shelves while she waited, and when she heard them come through the door, she came out of the kitchen with rubber gloves on. "Oh, baby, you're home! I was driving myself crazy with worry, waiting to hear something!" She waved the gloves with a sheepish smile. "I know it's so cliché for me to be cleaning your house for you, and I promise I'm not being all disapproving of the job you do keeping things clean—"

"It was a mess," Ivy said with a faint smile. "And thanks."

Arlene stripped off the wet gloves and wrung them in her hands a moment, looking for a place to put them. Antoine took them from her with a smile and carried them back into the kitchen while Arlene gave Ivy a hug.

"Did I hurt your shoulder?" she asked, pulling away quickly.

"It's pretty numb from the local anesthetic," Ivy assured her. "You didn't cook or anything, did you?"

"No, actually—" Arlene made a grimace that somehow worked its way into a sunny smile. "I was looking for you when Antoine called me. I have some really great news. At least, I hope you'll think it's great."

Ivy's stomach dropped. "You've met someone new."

Arlene's smile fell. "No, honey. I know that's what you'd expect from me—"

Antoine came out of the kitchen. "I've got to get back to the station, now that we're shorthanded. Take care of yourself, Hawk. I'll call you soon."

Ivy caught his hand as he moved past, giving it a squeeze. "Thanks for everything." After he let himself out the door, she turned to her mother and took her hand. "I shouldn't have interrupted. What's your good news?"

"Well, technically, it's really bad news, at least for your cousin Laurie."

Ivy tried to remember what was going on in Laurie's life these days. She was married, had two kids, and her husband was overseas somewhere in the army— "Oh, my God, Mom—has something happened to David?"

"Oh, no no no! No, he's fine as far as I know. It's Laurie—she got sideswiped the other day on the highway while she was driving home from the grocery store. Broke her left leg in two places and has to have a pin put in, but she's going to be okay. It's just a big problem for her, with those two kids to take care of. Your aunt Ellie already watches the kids for her when she has to go to the store or the doctor, but now she's going to have to watch after Laurie, too, and it's just going to be too much for her. So I'm heading down to Birmingham to help her out." Her mother finally took a breath.

"That's great," Ivy said, wishing she meant it as much as she wanted to. It would do her mother good to get away from Bitterwood for a while. Maybe she'd learn she liked it there in Birmingham. "You want me to keep a check on your house?"

"Actually, that's the other good news. You know how the town's been after me for a while to buy that property so they can expand Ridge Park up into the hills? I finally decided to say yes." Arlene looked equal parts excited and terrified. "Since I'm going to be in Birmingham at least six weeks, helping Ellie out, this might be a good time to sell the house and maybe look for somewhere else to live."

"Wow." Ivy stared at her mother, wondering how long she'd been sitting on that information. "I didn't even know you were considering it."

Arlene took Ivy's hands between hers. "I've been trying to talk to you for a few days, you know."

Ivy gave herself a mental kick. Her mother had left her messages telling her she needed to talk to her, and all Ivy had done was ignore her. "I'm sorry. This case has just been so crazy." *And I've been a selfish idiot.*

"I know you've despaired of me ever growin' up, Baby Bird, but it's time, don't you think? I'm not some young thing anymore, and I've finally realized I'm probably never going to find my Prince Charming. So it's time I find something else to do with my life." She patted Ivy's hand. "Maybe I'll like takin' care of Laurie and her babies. If I'm good at it, I could look at gettin' a job at a nursing home or something. Maybe down in Birmingham so I can be near Ellie and the girls. What would you think of that?"

Ivy felt a shredding sensation in the center of her chest, but she managed a genuine smile. "I think it would be good for you," she said. "I'd love for you to find something that makes you crazy happy, and I know you'd enjoy seeing Aunt Ellie more."

Arlene hugged her again, tears spilling down her cheeks. She wiped them away with a laugh. "Goodness, look at me, cryin' like a teenager who's leavin' home for the first time!"

"When are you going?"

"Well, I was going to leave this afternoon, but with you gettin' hurt—"

Ivy shook her head. "You go on to Birmingham, Mama. Drive safely, okay? Don't get pulled over."

"You sure?" Arlene asked as Ivy walked with her to the front door. "I can stay if you want me to."

"Laurie and those kids need you a lot more than I do."

Arlene cupped Ivy's cheek. "I don't reckon you've needed me in a long, long time, have you, Birdy?" She gave her a quick kiss on the forehead and walked down the porch steps and out to the Mustang convertible. Ivy watched from the doorway as her mother drove off, her graying hair fluttering in the wind.

She closed the door, crossed to the sofa and sat, picking up the throw pillow beside her. Breathing deeply, she smelled the lingering scent of her mother's favorite perfume.

I need you now, Mama. More than I ever thought I would.

An ache spread inside her, as if someone had just cracked open her heart and spilled out the contents. She closed her eyes against the sting of tears and told herself he was going to be okay. Yeah, life had just flung a great, steaming pile of manure her way, but she'd gotten through worse, hadn't she?

She'd been wanting her mother to find a new interest in life for years, after all. She certainly hadn't been happy at her job in a long while, ever since Glen Rayburn's promotion put him over the detective's division. So what if she ended up losing her badge? She'd find something else to do.

And Sutton Calhoun had left her before. It had hurt like hell, but she'd lived through it, hadn't she?

She heard the sound of a car engine pulling up outside, but she couldn't find the energy to get up and see who it was. Maybe her mother had left something. Or Antoine had thought to go to Bramlett Nurseries to retrieve her phone for her.

Footsteps hit the porch with a thud. Not her mother, she thought. So Antoine. She stood up to answer his knock.

But instead, a key scraped in the lock.

Instinct put her immediately on edge, and she backpedaled toward the chest of drawers where she kept her Glock. She dug in the pocket of her jeans for her key ring, cursing her sluggishness.

The door opened before she found the right key. Daylight outlined her visitor, turning him into a tall, lean silhouette she'd know anywhere.

"Sutton." A tingle of shock rippled through her body. She clutched the top of the chest of drawers, afraid she was about to tip right over.

He stood frozen in the doorway. "I didn't think you were here. There aren't any cars outside—"

"I thought you'd already left town."

He shook his head. "I've got about an hour before I have to meet the chopper."

"Oh. You came for your things." She started toward the hallway. "Are they still in the guest room?"

She heard the door slam shut and a rush of footsteps behind her. As she turned, Sutton was right there, his arms snaking out to wrap around her waist and pull her close.

His mouth covered hers in a slow, deep kiss that sent her head spinning until she felt drunk with need. She clung to him, her fingers digging into his sides to keep her from falling, and she matched him kiss for kiss.

Dragging his mouth away from hers, he planted soft kisses along the curve of her cheek until his lips brushed her ear. "Tell me to stay."

"Wait." She tried to clear her head, but his mouth was sparking fires along her nervous system, making it hard to do anything but feel.

"Just say it, Ivy. Tell me to stay."

She pushed against his chest, tearing herself from his grasp. Light-headed, she stumbled to the sofa and sat heavily.

Sutton sat next to her, grasping her hands between his. "I came here to tell you goodbye, but I can't do it. Not this time. Please tell me to stay."

She couldn't think. She had to think, had to make a good decision, but he was sitting there, big and gorgeous and hotter than the August sun, and all she wanted was to wrap herself around him and make good and sure he never left her again.

"Antoine said—" Her voice broke. She cleared her throat and started again. "Antoine said you had to fly overseas to handle something."

"I'll quit my job." He caressed her hands, his hazel eyes wild as he pinned her with his desperate gaze. "Say the words, Ivy. Just say them. Tell me to stay, and I'll call Jesse right now."

She shook her head. "You can't quit."

He stared at her a moment, his hands falling still. Then he let go of her hands. "Okay. Okay, then."

He got up, his movements ungainly. Drunken. He staggered toward the door.

"You can't quit because one of us is going to need a job."

He went still, his hand covering the doorknob.

"I'm probably going to be booted from the police department." She stood up and walked toward him. "My mother just informed me she's selling her house and moving to Birmingham, at least for six weeks but maybe for good."

Sutton turned around to look at her, his eyes blazing.

"There's nothing to keep me here. No reason for me to tell you to stay." She closed the last few inches of distance between them, laying her hands on his chest, her pulse thundering in her ears as she saw the truth in his eyes, a truth that had lived in her heart since she was a young girl in love with the boy next door. "So take me with you."

He cradled her face between his palms. "I can't take you to Iraq."

"So I'll wait for you in Alabama."

He kissed her forehead, the touch almost reverent. She wrapped her arms around his waist and melted against him. "I love you, Ivy Hawkins. I've loved you for half my life. It just took me until now to realize it."

"I knew it fourteen years ago," she murmured against the side of his neck. "I just never thought I'd get to tell you."

He stroked her hair, brushing his lips to her temple. "Know what I think? I think it was no coincidence that we grew up together on Smoky Ridge. We were meant to find each other back then, and become friends when we both needed someone to trust." He tipped her head back, making her look at him. "I remember, when Jesse told me about this case in Bitterwood, I thought, 'What are the odds I'd be going back there after all this time?' But now it seems so clear I was supposed to come back. To you."

"You really believe that?" she asked, both thrilled and terrified by the idea that something out there had brought them back together.

"Don't you?"

She did, she realized with surprise. It sounded crazy and fanciful. It sounded like something her mother would believe. But she knew it was true, deep in her soul where a part of Sutton had always remained, long after he was physically gone. A part of her had always believed he'd be back for that piece of his soul. "Yeah," she said. "I do."

He hugged her close, his embrace both heated and oddly gentle, a perfect melding of their platonic past and their passionate present. She kissed the side of his neck, making him groan.

"I'm going to quit my job at Cooper Security, Ivy. Everything I want in this world anymore is right here in Bitterwood." His voice was thick with need. "I guess I've missed this place more than I ever wanted to admit."

"Are you sure?"

He brushed a kiss against her forehead. "Yeah. You're here."

She felt her insides melt into a hot puddle. "Your dad's still here. All that history—"

"Leavin' this place didn't change that history," he murmured against her temple. "I am who I am. I come from the people I come from. All I did by running away was let the people around these parts think there's only one kind of Calhoun. I'd like to challenge that notion."

"I guess, if I'm honest with myself, I never really wanted to leave here. I could have gone anytime. I was using my mother as an excuse." She'd realized that embarrassing bit of truth while watching her mother drive away. "Smoky Ridge has a way of getting into your bones."

"It does," he agreed, his tone serious.

"So if you quit your job, how do you plan to make a living?" She arched a look at him. "I'm a liberated woman, but that doesn't mean I plan to support you while you sleep all day. Too damned much of that going on in these hills as it is."

"I'll find something to do here. I have skills, you know."

She shot him a wicked smile. "I'm countin' on that, Calhoun."

He laughed and kissed her again, sending fire pouring through her veins once more. If she didn't watch out, she'd become completely addicted to his touch.

She stepped out of his embrace but held on to his hands. "When do you have to meet the helicopter?"

He glanced at his watch, his expression alarmed. "Too damned soon. I'd better get moving. I still need to pack."

"Why don't I take you to meet the helicopter? You can leave your truck here until you're back."

"Delilah's coming to take my place," he told her as they went to gather the rest of his belongings. "She'll be without wheels, so I reckon she'll be borrowing the truck until she's done with the mop-up of the case. But she can bring you back here."

They walked together out to his truck. He opened the passenger door, stopping her from getting in with a kiss. "Are you really sure about this? I know it's all happening so fast and I'm not exactly being my usual practical self about things—"

"I'm sure," she said with a smile. "I love you, Sutton Calhoun. I've loved you for years. And I'm damned well going to love you the rest of my life, so you'd better just get used to it."

"I'll do my best," he said with a wicked grin, and bent to kiss her again.

Epilogue

Rachel Davenport's silver Honda Accord sat parked next to her father's old Volvo in the back lot of the trucking company. Most of the other employees had left at six, but George Davenport had always been a workaholic, from what Seth had learned over his time with the company, and his terminal cancer had only driven him to work that much harder, as time ran out on him.

Rachel's mother had been gone since she was a teenager, and her father was fading away in front of her eyes. Now Mark Bramlett had ripped away four more people she was close to, including a woman who had almost been a second mother to her. And he'd done it deliberately, with Rachel's heart in his crosshairs, because someone else had paid him to do it.

Seth wanted to know who.

His cell phone rang, giving him a small jolt. The name on the display evoked a grimace. Adam Brand. Mr. FBI himself.

He answered. "Yeah?"

"Hammond, it's Brand." The voice on the other end was deep, with a drawl that placed him squarely south of the

Mason-Dixon Line. Brand was from Georgia, and over a decade in Washington hadn't erased his drawl.

"So my phone says."

"Did you know your sister's on her way there?"

Seth arched an eyebrow. "Yeah, but how did you know? Never mind, need to know and all that." After three years of doing jobs for Brand, Seth had grown used to working with only half the information he'd have liked to have. The secrecy wasn't something he'd enjoyed, exactly, but he'd put up with it in order to have a chance to do something decent for a change.

But he wasn't inclined to do more jobs for Brand after the last one.

"I have another job for you."

Seth's gaze slid back toward Rachel Davenport's Honda. "I told you after last time, I'm not interested in doing any more jobs for you and the feds. Damned near lost my head that time."

"This one shouldn't be as dangerous," Brand said firmly. "And you're already uniquely positioned to do what I need."

"Yeah?" The back door of Davenport Trucking opened and two people emerged, one gray and hunched, the other tall, slender and outwardly composed. But Seth knew if he were close enough to look into her blue eyes, he'd see Rachel Davenport's fear and pain. She was trying so hard to be strong for her father and for herself.

And someone was trying damned hard to knock her down until she couldn't get up again.

"I need you to find out who hired Mark Bramlett to kill the people around Rachel Davenport," Brand said.

"How do you even know about that?" Seth asked, suspicious.

"I just spent a half hour on a satellite phone with Jesse Cooper," Brand answered. "He's apparently been talking to Sutton Calhoun, who told his boss everything that happened today. And given that surveillance job you did for us in Alabama last year—"

Phantom pain pricked his scalp at the mention of that particular job. "Not smart to remind me of that job again, Brand."

"You're good at lying low and getting information. That's what we need in this case. I want someone who can keep an eye on Rachel Davenport and her family without drawing attention."

"What's it to you? Sutton Calhoun solved the murders. Isn't that all the FBI should give a damn about?"

"The FBI isn't involved in this one, Seth. This is for me."

That was new. "Could I get arrested for any of this?"

"Not if you don't break any laws."

Easier said than done, Seth thought.

"Do you want the job?"

Seth looked across the parking lot. George Davenport insisted on driving himself while he still could, but it wouldn't be long until he'd have to give in to his growing weakness. Rachel watched him drive out of the parking lot before she unlocked the Honda and slid behind the wheel.

He waited for her to start the car. But she just sat there a moment, her posture ramrod straight.

"Hammond?" Adam Brand prodded.

Rachel crumpled forward slowly, terribly, and buried

her face in her hands. Her shoulders shook, and Seth felt a dart of pain in his own chest.

"I'll do it," he said aloud, his eyes never leaving the spectacle of grief playing out in front of him. "I'll take the job."

* * * * *

*Award-winning author Paula Graves's brand-new miniseries, BITTERWOOD, P.D., continues next month with THE SMOKY MOUNTAIN MIST.
Look for it wherever
Harlequin Intrigue books are sold!*

COMING NEXT MONTH from Harlequin® Intrigue®
AVAILABLE JUNE 18, 2013

#1431 OUTLAW LAWMAN
The Marshals of Maverick County
Delores Fossen
A search for a killer brings Marshal Harlan McKinney and investigative journalist Caitlyn Barnes face-to-face not only with their painful pasts but with a steamy attraction that just won't die. Only together can they defeat the murderer who lures them back to a Texas ranch for a midnight showdown.

#1432 THE SMOKY MOUNTAIN MIST
Bitterwood P.D.
Paula Graves
Who is trying to make heiress Rachel Davenport think she's going crazy? And why? Former bad boy Seth Hammond will put his life—and his heart—on the line to find out.

#1433 TRIGGERED
Covert Cowboys, Inc.
Elle James
When ex-cop Ben Harding is hired to protect a woman and her child, he must learn to trust in himself and his abilities to defend truth and justice...and allow himself to love again.

#1434 FEARLESS
Corcoran Team
HelenKay Dimon
Undercover operative Davis Weeks lost everything when he picked work over his personal life. But now he gets a second chance when Lara Barton, the woman he's always loved, turns to him for help.

#1435 CARRIE'S PROTECTOR
Rebecca York
Carrie Mitchell is terrified to find herself in the middle of a terrorist plot...and in the arms of her tough-guy bodyguard, Wyatt Hawk.

#1436 FOR THE BABY'S SAKE
Beverly Long
Detective Sawyer Montgomery needs testimony from Liz Mayfield's pregnant teenage client, who is unexpectedly missing. Can Sawyer and Liz find the teen in time to save her and her baby?

You can find more information on upcoming Harlequin®
titles, free excerpts and more at www.Harlequin.com.

HICNM0613

REQUEST YOUR FREE BOOKS!
2 FREE NOVELS PLUS 2 FREE GIFTS!

HARLEQUIN®

INTRIGUE®

BREATHTAKING ROMANTIC SUSPENSE

YES! Please send me 2 FREE Harlequin Intrigue® novels and my 2 FREE gifts (gifts are worth about $10). After receiving them, if I don't wish to receive any more books, I can return the shipping statement marked "cancel." If I don't cancel, I will receive 6 brand-new novels every month and be billed just $4.74 per book in the U.S. or $5.24 per book in Canada. That's a savings of at least 14% off the cover price! It's quite a bargain! Shipping and handling is just 50¢ per book in the U.S. and 75¢ per book in Canada.* I understand that accepting the 2 free books and gifts places me under no obligation to buy anything. I can always return a shipment and cancel at any time. Even if I never buy another book, the two free books and gifts are mine to keep forever.

182/382 HDN F42N

Name	(PLEASE PRINT)	

Address		Apt. #

City	State/Prov.	Zip/Postal Code

Signature (if under 18, a parent or guardian must sign)

Mail to the **Harlequin® Reader Service:**
IN U.S.A.: P.O. Box 1867, Buffalo, NY 14240-1867
IN CANADA: P.O. Box 609, Fort Erie, Ontario L2A 5X3
**Are you a subscriber to Harlequin Intrigue books
and want to receive the larger-print edition?
Call 1-800-873-8635 or visit www.ReaderService.com.**

* Terms and prices subject to change without notice. Prices do not include applicable taxes. Sales tax applicable in N.Y. Canadian residents will be charged applicable taxes. Offer not valid in Quebec. This offer is limited to one order per household. Not valid for current subscribers to Harlequin Intrigue books. All orders subject to credit approval. Credit or debit balances in a customer's account(s) may be offset by any other outstanding balance owed by or to the customer. Please allow 4 to 6 weeks for delivery. Offer available while quantities last.

Your Privacy—The Harlequin® Reader Service is committed to protecting your privacy. Our Privacy Policy is available online at www.ReaderService.com or upon request from the Harlequin Reader Service.

We make a portion of our mailing list available to reputable third parties that offer products we believe may interest you. If you prefer that we not exchange your name with third parties, or if you wish to clarify or modify your communication preferences, please visit us at www.ReaderService.com/consumerchoice or write to us at Harlequin Reader Service Preference Service, P.O. Box 9062, Buffalo, NY 14269. Include your complete name and address.

HI13R

Looking for another great Western read?
Jump into action with

TRIGGERED

by

Elle James

the first installment in the Covert Cowboys, Inc. series.

*When mysterious threats are made on the lives of
Kate Langsdon and her young daughter, only decorated
former Austin police officer Ben Harding is willing to
protect them at any cost.*

The warmth of his hands on her arms sent shivers throughout her body. "Really, it's fine," she said, even as she let him maneuver her to sit on the arm of the couch.

Ben squatted, pulled the tennis shoe off her foot and removed her sock. "I had training as a first responder on the Austin police force. Let me be the judge."

Kate held her breath as he lifted her foot and turned it to inspect the ankle, his fingers grazing over her skin.

"See? Just bumped it. It'll be fine in a minute." She cursed inwardly at her breathlessness. A man's hands on her ankle shouldn't send her into a tailspin. Ben Harding was a trained professional—touching a woman's ankle meant nothing other than a concern for health and safety. Nothing more.

Then why was she breathing like a teenager on her first date? Kate bent to slide her foot back into her shoe, biting hard on her lip to keep from crying out at the pain. When she turned toward him she could feel the warmth of his breath fan across her cheek.

"You should put a little ice on that," he said, his tone as smooth as warm syrup.

Ice was exactly what she needed. To chill her natural reaction to a handsome man, paid to help and protect her, not touch, hold or kiss her.

Kate jumped up and moved away from Ben and his gentle fingers. "I should get back outside. No telling what Lily is up to."

Ben caught her arm as she passed him. "You felt it, too, didn't you?"

Kate fought the urge to lean into him and sniff the musky scent of male. Four years was a long time to go without a man. "I don't know what you're talking about."

Ben held her arm a moment longer, then let go. "You're right. We should check on Lily."

Kate hurried for the door. Just as she crossed the threshold into the south Texas sunshine, a frightened scream made her racing heart stop.

Don't miss the dramatic conclusion to
TRIGGERED by Elle James.

Available July 2013, only from Harlequin Intrigue.

Copyright © 2013 by Harlequin Books S.A.

SADDLE UP AND READ 'EM!

This summer, get your fix of Western reads and pick up a cowboy from the SUSPENSE category in July!

OUTLAW LAWMAN by Delores Fossen,
The Marshals of Maverick County
Harlequin Intrigue

TRIGGERED by Elle James,
Covert Cowboys, Inc.
Harlequin Intrigue

*Look for these great Western reads AND MORE,
available wherever books are sold or visit*
www.Harlequin.com/Westerns

SUART0613SUSP